DEATH
on the
CARDS

DEATH
on the
CARDS

Richard Grayson

St. Martin's Press
New York

Library of Congress Cataloging-in-Publication Data

Grayson, Richard.
    Death on the cards / by Richard Grayson.
        p.   cm.
    ISBN 0-312-01758-8
    I. Title.
PR6057.R55D413   1988
823'.914—dc19   87-38256
                                                                 CIP

First published in Great Britain by Macmillan London Limited.

First U.S. Edition

10 9 8 7 6 5 4 3 2 1

BL BL   MAY 15 '89

1

As the first light picked out its spires and towers, Gautier, standing on Pont Neuf, was astonished, as he had often been before, by the transformation in Paris. It was as though each new dawn brought a rebirth, leaving the city free of the violence and vice and corruption which disfigured it by night. Even the Seine flowed soundlessly beneath its silent bridges, as though reluctant to disturb a sleep of innocence.

The smell of violence and fear still hung on him, for he had spent most of the night in Pigalle, lying in wait for a man who was suspected of murder, following a tip-off which, like so many others, had proved false. The murder was the second in Pigalle within four nights. In a *quartier* where stabbings and brutal assaults were a nocturnal commonplace, that statistic might not be thought unusual, but the two killings had certain features in common: the manner of their execution was identical, a single upward thrust with a broad-bladed knife, expertly placed; and both seemed to be without motive. Afraid that the two might be forerunners of a string of gruesome murders like those committed in London by the maniac whom the English had christened Jack the Ripper, the Sûreté had started an investigation. Gautier had been sent to Pigalle and had so far learnt nothing of any significance.

An excellent breakfast in one of the cafés around Les Halles, which catered for porters from the markets nearby, had helped him to forget the frustration of the night, and now, after reporting back at Sûreté headquarters which overlooked the Seine on Quai des Orfèvres, he was on his way to his apartment on the Left Bank. And as he so often did, he had stopped as he was crossing the river to lean on the parapet of the bridge and look at the water.

Before long Paris would begin to stir itself. The streets would gradually fill; with workmen whose *métier* demanded an early start, with priests hurrying to prepare their churches for the first Mass of the day, with tradesmen selling provisions from their horse-drawn vans, each shouting his distinctive cry and bringing out servants from the houses around to buy milk, bread and vegetables for the day. But now both the city and the river were still silent and deserted.

Then Gautier saw a rowing boat pull out into the middle of the river. It appeared to have come from around the stern of a houseboat which was moored some two or three hundred metres down along the Left Bank, almost opposite Sûreté headquarters. The houseboat, Gautier knew, was owned by a wealthy Greek businessman and it was large enough to require a crew of a captain and five sailors. The man in the rowing boat, though, was not wearing a sailor's uniform but a brown suit and brown derby hat, a form of dress common enough in the boulevards, but one seldom favoured by those who went boating, whether as their livelihood or for pleasure.

With accomplished, economical strokes the man in the brown suit crossed the river diagonally and rowed along beside Quai des Orfèvres until he disappeared from view beyond Pont St Michel. Gautier looked at the houseboat and noticed that since the last time he had seen it, several months previously, the hull had been repainted and the awning over the deck, under which passengers could recline in sunny weather, had been changed. The former awning of red and white striped canvas had been replaced by one in gold and white and all the brass fittings of the boat seemed freshly burnished. That probably meant that the houseboat was about to leave on another cruise, down the Seine and along the coast to Normandy or Brittany, stopping at any harbour which the owner felt might offer a good dinner, a casino or some other distraction for his guests.

Suddenly, as he was looking at the houseboat, its whole stern appeared to disintegrate, fragments of wood, metal and canvas flying upwards and outwards, each tracing its own trajectory. Only as they began to fall, seconds later it seemed, did the roar of the explosion carry across the water.

Behind it followed a long moment's hushed silence. Then debris began to clatter on to the embankment beside the boat and to flop into the water. From the eaves and ledges of the buildings across Quai des Grands-Augustins birds flew up in fright, filling the air with the agitated thrashing of their wings.

Running across the bridge and along beside the river, Gautier reached the houseboat at the same time as a caretaker who came out of a building opposite it pulling his trousers on over his nightshirt. His wife, a shawl around her shoulders and paper curlers in her hair, stood frightened, watching from the doorway. The stern of the houseboat was badly damaged, with a jagged hole in the hull, which fortunately seemed to be above the water-line, and another in the deck, through which smoke was billowing.

'Was there anyone on board?' Gautier asked the caretaker.

'Two sailors, I suppose. The crew take it in turn to sleep on board and guard the boat while it's moored here.'

'Ask your wife to telephone the local police commissariat.' Gautier knew that the building from which the man had come housed a government department and would therefore have a telephone. 'Tell them an ambulance is needed and the fire brigade, quickly.'

7

'I'll have to do it myself. My wife doesn't understand the telephone.'

The man hurried away and Gautier swiftly crossed the small gangplank which led from the quayside on to the houseboat. He remembered something of the layout of the vessel from his previous visits to it and knew that the saloon, the dining saloon, the owner's study and passenger cabins were all to be found in the middle and the bows, while the engine room and crew's quarters were in the stern. Below decks the passageway leading to the crew's quarters was full of smoke. Holding a handkerchief over his nose and mouth he tried to find his way along it but was forced back, choking and with streaming eyes.

The fire which, he suspected, was in the engine room of the boat would have to be extinguished before anyone who might have been injured in the explosion could be reached. There would be a hose on board, used for washing down the decks, but Gautier had no idea where it would be stowed nor how it could be connected to the boat's pumps. In any event the pumps themselves might well have been damaged by the explosion. Going back on deck, he found that a score of people had gathered on the quay, all of them from buildings nearby and most of them straight out of their beds. He sent some of them for pails and others for lengths of rope with which to lower the pails over the side of the houseboat. Presently he had a squad working, filling their pails from the river and tossing the water into the hole in the deck.

Their efforts did not even contain the fire. The smoke grew denser as it billowed out, with tongues of flame shooting upwards through it, and Gautier was relieved when a clanging of bells and the sound of hooves on the cobbles told him that a fire engine, drawn by a team of horses, was arriving. The firemen took charge and, as soon as the fire was under control, two of them went below with axes to cut a passage through the wreckage which the explosion

8

had created in the stern of the boat below deck. After a time one of them returned.

'Has the ambulance arrived?' he asked Gautier. 'We've found the two sailors.'

'How are they?'

'Both dead. The place is a mangled wreck down there.'

'Have you any idea of what might have caused the explosion?'

The fireman shrugged his shoulders. 'We'll have to wait for the experts to examine the damage, but there's no doubt in my mind. It can only have been a bomb.'

The Café Corneille was beginning to fill up when Gautier arrived there later that morning. Of the small circle of friends who met regularly in the café only Froissart, a bookseller from the Left Bank, was already there and Gautier joined him at his table. The Café Corneille did not draw its clientele from any one profession or *métier*. One could find cafés in Paris for bankers and diamond merchants and journalists and even circus performers, but the only attributes which habitués of the Café Corneille seemed to have in common were lively minds and a respect for the views of other people. When Gautier reached Froissart he saw that he was reading a copy of *Le Monde*.

'You had better hide that paper when Duthrey arrives,' Gautier told him. Duthrey was one of their friends, a journalist who worked for *Figaro*. 'Or he'll accuse you of disloyalty.'

'I've already read *Figaro*,' Froissart replied. 'I only bought *Le Monde* to read what that charlatan Astrux has to say. *Le Monde* is carrying a long interview with him today.'

'Astrux? What is his latest prophecy? That we are to be invaded by men from Mars?'

'Nothing so precise as that; the collapse of the Entente Cordiale, an assassination and a major political scandal which will bring the Government down.'

9

'One does not have to be clairvoyant to predict the fall of a French government.'

'No,' Froissart agreed. 'They succumb as easily as the virginity of a convent educated girl.'

Astrux was the professional name of a self-professed astrologer and clairvoyant who was very much in vogue at that time. Wealthy Parisians would pay handsome fees for consultations with him, bankers and stockbrokers were supposed to be guided by his predictions when making their business decisions and ladies slavishly followed his advice on any matter from the colour of their dresses to the choice of names for their pet dogs. Astrux was a name he had devised from the initials of his real name, Achille de Saint-Trucheron.

'At least he is now being circumspect in what he says about the President,' Gautier remarked.

'For the time being perhaps, but he'll never forgive Loubet. He took it as a personal insult and an affront to his dignity that anyone should take him to court.'

'Even the President?'

'Especially the President.'

About two years previously Astrux had published a prediction which might have been considered to imply that the President of the Republic had been taking bribes. He was immediately charged with criminal libel, found guilty and sentenced to a year in prison and a heavy fine. However, the President had exercised clemency: the prison sentence had been lifted but the fine doubled. The sensation of the trial had not damaged Astrux's reputation; rather the reverse, and the number of Parisians pressing for consultations and horoscopes and mystic seances had doubled overnight.

Gautier and Froissart were still talking about Astrux when two more of their circle arrived. One was an elderly judge, a man whose crusty manner and astringent comments on the manners of the day concealed a shrewd brain and an inherent kindness. The other was the deputy

10

for Val-de-Marne. They joined in the discussion. No one seriously believed that Astrux was able to foretell the future, but they conceded that he was remarkably skilful in turning notoriety to his advantage. His name had been linked with many scandals: stories of black masses and satanism and of young girl disciples with whom his relationship was a good deal less than supernatural. Each scandal, reported in obsessive detail by the press, only appeared to add to Astrux's lustre. He was invited to the salons of the most fashionable hostesses in Paris and it was hinted that he was consulted by members of the royal houses of Europe whenever they visited the city.

From the notoriety of Astrux their conversation broadened inevitably into a discussion of French society and the future of France – inevitably, because many thinking Frenchmen saw in the behaviour of men like Astrux a symptom of the decline in morality which they believed was undermining the country.

'We are living in the twentieth century,' Froissart remarked. 'How can people believe in fortune-tellers?'

'Don't talk to me about the twentieth century!' the judge exclaimed. 'What has it brought us? A collapse in morality, a slide towards anarchy.'

'The century is still young. It will bring progress, one can be sure of that. We will have new inventions to make life more comfortable for us.'

'Like the automobiles which fill our streets with noise and our lungs with their loathsome fumes?'

'What I deplore,' Froissart said, 'is that elegance is vanishing from life. In the nineties France led the world in fashion, style and taste as well as in art and culture.'

'She still does. France is the centre of the civilised world. Everyone comes to Paris – English milords, American millionaires, German composers, Swedish philosophers.'

'And what have they brought us? Homosexuality.'

11

They began to talk about the homosexuality of both sexes which was being reported in the press, and that led to a discussion of free thinking and the growing agitation for women's rights. Gautier listened, making no more than an occasional comment, not because he did not have opinions of his own to contribute, but because the conversation seemed to be veering towards politics. Men went to cafés to exchange opinions on the matters of the day, very often passionately and heatedly. Some cafés had been breeding grounds for discontent and subversion and the Government had been known to send in spies and agents provocateurs to identify trouble-makers. Gautier was secretly proud that the habitués of the Café Corneille trusted him enough to accept him as an equal, talking freely in front of him, but he considered it prudent to avoid becoming involved in political arguments.

'A pity our friend Duthrey is not here,' he remarked. 'He has strong views on the decline in morality in our country.'

'It isn't too late,' the judge said. 'Unless my eyes deceive me he is just arriving.'

The judge was not mistaken, for at that moment Duthrey came into the café. The journalist from *Figaro* was a small man, inclined to stoutness, but the tailor who made his frock coats cut them in a way which concealed his embonpoint and enhanced his air of quiet dignity. His friends in the Café Corneille often teased him, though never un-kindly, for his unshakeable belief in the sanctity of marriage and family life and for his insistence on following the same precise and unchanging daily routine. That morning the pattern had been broken and Duthrey was not pleased.

'It really is too bad!' he complained, looking at his pocket-watch as he came up to their table. 'I'm more than twenty minutes late!'

'What cataclysmic piece of news was it that kept you at your desk?' the deputy for Val-de-Marne teased him. 'Has the Pope caught a cold in the head?'

Duthrey snorted. 'One of my colleagues was sent out to cover some trifling incident on the river and I've been doing his work. It's scandalous that we do not have enough staff to run the paper properly.'

'What was the incident?'

'An explosion on a houseboat. You will have seen the one. It's tied up alongside Quai des Grands-Augustins.'

'It was more than a trifling incident,' Gautier told him quietly. 'Two sailors were killed in that explosion.'

'I had no idea! What a terrible thing.'

'You were not to know.' Gautier could see that Duthrey was upset and ashamed at his thoughtless remark. 'I only know about the explosion because I saw it happen.'

The other men around the table looked at Gautier enquiringly, wishing to know how he had come to witness the explosion but not wanting to question him. Normally he never mentioned any police investigations on which he was working to his friends at the Café Corneille, and neither did they. This time he could see no harm in telling them about the explosion, for what little he knew would soon be public knowledge when it was reported in the newspapers. So he told the others how he had come to be on Pont Neuf that morning and what he had seen.

'I was passing the houseboat on my way to the Assemblée Nationale this morning,' the deputy said, 'and I stopped for a moment to watch the firemen who were still trying to clear the debris. Many of the windows in buildings nearby had been shattered.'

'Was anyone injured besides the two sailors?'

'It appears not.'

'One of them was truly a victim of fate,' the deputy remarked. 'They say it was not his turn to sleep on board the houseboat, but he had agreed to so that another of the crew could attend a wedding of a relative in Calais.'

'To whom does the boat belong?' Froissart asked.

'The Greek armament salesman, Paul Valanis.'

'To have a boat like that built for one is just vulgar ostentation,' Duthrey said indignantly. 'They tell me there is every conceivable luxury on board, even a grand piano. It's a miniature floating palace in execrable taste.'

'What must the poor in Paris think when they see it tied up in the Seine?' the judge commented.

Paul Valanis had arrived in Paris four or five years previously as the accredited representative of Lydon-Walters, the British armaments firm. Selling field-guns and rifles and machine-guns was a lucrative business, particularly in France where the Government was determined to build up the country's military strength and so avoid any repetition of the humiliation which Bismarck and the Prussians had inflicted on the French only three decades previously. Valanis, backed with the resources of his company, had built a huge house in Avenue du Bois where he entertained Government ministers and leading figures in Paris society. He was reputed to be as rich as the Rothschilds and a good deal more generous, especially to ladies.

Gautier did not tell the others that he knew something of Valanis's past, most of it discreditable, for only two years previously he had been in charge of an investigation into the murder of an art dealer from Montmartre which had involved one of the leading hostesses of Paris, the Princesse de Caramond, at that time Valanis's mistress. The origins of Valanis were obscure but he had faced criminal prosecutions in both Greece and Turkey on charges which ranged from living on the immoral earnings of women to smuggling and the misappropriation of rifles from the Turkish army. On every occasion he had contrived to avoid prison, even though in Turkey the Minister of War and two of his subordinates had been executed for their part in the affair of the rifles. Gautier had found it hard to understand how a man with such a record had come to be appointed to represent one of the largest armament companies in the world, but then selling arms, he supposed, was a

14

business which attracted scoundrels. In any event Valanis had been accepted by the French authorities as a man of good standing.

'How on earth did the man get permission to moor his boat in the centre of Paris?' Froissart asked.

'He has friends in high places,' the deputy replied.

'Isn't it a coincidence that we should have been talking about Astrux earlier?' the judge remarked.

'Where is the coincidence?'

'Valanis was one of the people who, Astrux suggested, had been bribing the President of the Republic.'

'He did not name Valanis surely?' Gautier asked.

'His prediction was read out in court. Do you remember? The President would be forced to resign, he foretold, for being too responsive to disarming gifts from a man from Macedonia. "Disarming gifts. A man from Macedonia." Who else could Astrux have meant but the Greek arms salesman, Valanis?'

2

When a maid showed Gautier into the drawing room of her apartment in rue de Miromesnil, a few minutes before the time when he had promised to call for her, Michelle Le Tellier was ready dressed and waiting. The blue evening gown which Paquin had designed for her had a décolletage which would arouse any man's admiration, just as her diamond and sapphire necklace and earrings would provoke most women's envy. Excitement and a hint of impatience had added colour to her cheeks and a restless sparkle to her eyes.

'How do I look?' she asked him, holding out one of her white gloved hands to be kissed.

'Enchanting,' Gautier replied truthfully.

'This gown isn't too young for me? Too virginal?'

'Absolutely not. It's perfect.'

One could sympathise with her anxiety. Madame Le Tellier was a widow whose husband, the editor of the newspaper *La Parole*, had been shot and killed by a young woman several months previously. His murder had been one in a series of incidents planned by a group of conspirators in an attempt to bring down the Government and seize power themselves, a plot which had been discovered and frustrated by Gautier. He had met Madame Le Tellier during the course of his investigation into the murder and they had formed a friendship which before long had slipped into intimacy. From time to time he would dine with her in her apartment, secretly, for by the strict conventions of French society a widow must remain in mourning for her husband, always wearing black, never leaving her home without a chaperone and never entertaining guests or accepting invitations.

Now at last the period of mourning was over. During the last week she had been out twice, once to a dinner party and once to the opera, both times escorted by Gautier, and that evening they were going to a soirée in the salon of Madame Léontine Mauberge where, for the first time since her husband's death, she would meet and be seen by many of the leading figures in society.

Madame Mauberge's home was in Faubourg St-Germain, the district just south of the Seine and to the east of Esplanade des Invalides which had escaped destruction when Haussmann, commissioned by Napoleon III, had pulled down most of the centre of Paris to build a city of broad avenues and majestic boulevards. Old aristocratic families which had also been fortunate enough to escape destruction during the Revolution had lived in that area for centuries. Madame Mauberge was not an aristocrat but her husband, a wealthy financier, had bought a dilapidated seventeenth-century house, had it beautifully restored and filled it with fine furniture and works of art.

The salon which she held once a week was one of the three or four leading bourgeois salons in Paris. Each salon had its coterie of celebrities who attended regularly – authors, poets and musicians – and in attracting to her salon the 'lions' of the day Madame Mauberge had to compete with Madame Arman de Caillavet, the mistress of Anatole France, and Madame Geneviève Straus, the widow of the composer Bizet, who had married for a second time, a wealthy lawyer. France himself had been one of her guests, though not often as Madame de Caillavet was possessive and jealous, as well as the novelist Pierre Loti and the poet and aesthete Comte Robert de Montesquieu. When Michelle Le Tellier and he arrived in Madame Mauberge's drawing room that evening, the only celebrity

17

Gautier recognised was Renée de Saules, who at one time many had thought to be the greatest poetess in France, if not in Europe.

Madame Mauberge was a woman of about sixty, with billowing red hair and a face so heavily painted that it might have been a mask used in a medieval miracle play. Her smile, though ready, was tight and pinched and one had the feeling that if she laughed the mask might crack and fall to pieces.

When Gautier was presented to her she exclaimed, 'Monsieur Gautier! At last you have consented to honour my little salon!'

'You flatter me, Madame. I am only too conscious that I do not merit an invitation.' Gautier did not add that he had never before received one.

'Fiddlesticks! All Paris is talking of your wit and intelligence, not to mention your reputation with the ladies.' She tapped him playfully on the arm with her fan. 'I shall steal you from Michelle for a tête-à-tête conversation later.'

'Be careful, Léontine,' Michelle le Tellier said. 'No woman is safe with him!'

'I am counting on that.'

More guests arrived and had to be welcomed and as Michelle and he moved away Gautier said, 'Madame Mauberge is clearly a woman of taste and discernment.'

'Don't let her praise go to your head. She mistook you for one of my other beaux.'

'That's unkind,' Gautier said and laughed, but he had the feeling it may have been true.

The elegance and style of the furniture and works of art in the room where the soirée was being held were difficult to appreciate because, as in most bourgeois drawing rooms, every spare corner was taken up with palms in huge pots and vases full of flowers while the mantelpiece and the tops of the grand piano and of every table

18

were covered with ornaments, mementoes and bric-à-brac. Faded sepia photographs in heavy silver frames stood next to exquisite eighteenth-century miniatures, a brass model of the Eiffel Tower commemorating the day in 1889 on which it had been officially opened stood uncomfortably among porcelain from Sèvres and delicate jewelled eggs created by Cartier. Elsewhere Gautier saw picture post-cards of an unbelievable banality, a death mask of Balzac, paperweights, snuffboxes and glass bowls, some valuable, others trivial and worthless. Although the room was easily large enough to hold the guests who had already arrived, as well as those who were expected, it seemed suffocatingly overcrowded.

After leaving their hostess, Michelle and Gautier mingled with other guests and presently they found themselves with Monsieur de Saules and his wife. Gautier had met the banker two or three years previously when investigating the death of an abbé who had been their family confessor and parish priest. At that time Renée de Saules had retired from both literary life and society and was living very nearly as a recluse. Tonight she looked pale, as suited a poetess, but was far more animated than she had been when they had last met.

'Renée!' Michelle exclaimed. 'How delightful it is to have you back among us!'

Madame de Saules smiled, mischievously it seemed to Gautier. 'I was about to make the same remark to you.'

'And it's wonderful that you have started writing again.'

'Not all the critics would agree with you. They think my muse is dead and should not have been resurrected.'

'Nonsense! Some of the poems in your new book are beautiful; as good as anything you have ever written. I sent out for a copy the day it was published.'

'And you, Monsieur Gautier,' Monsieur de Saules said smiling. 'Have you also helped to swell the sales of this poor poet?'

19

'I am ashamed to say not, Monsieur, but I will buy one tomorrow.'

'You will not!' Madame de Saules said. 'I will have an inscribed copy sent round to you.'

'And an invitation to our next soirée.' One could sense that Monsieur de Saules was delighted by his wife's return to a normal social life and was doing all he could to make sure that she would enjoy it.

'I find it disconcerting,' Madame de Saules commented, looking around the room, 'that there are so many people here whom I don't even know.'

'Even I notice that,' Michelle agreed, 'after only a few months. For example who is that distinguished-looking man with the grey beard?'

'He's a Norwegian philosopher named Thorndaal,' Monsieur de Saules replied. 'A new arrival in Paris and a charming man, but so erudite that few people can understand his conversation.'

'And that slim man with the monocle?'

'The Honourable James Dew; an Englishman over in Paris for the races,' Gautier said. He did not add that the Sûreté had been advised to keep an eye on Dew who was suspected of a major swindle in which a London bank had been defrauded of half-a-million pounds.

Gautier was wishing that he could sit down. He had managed to fit in only a couple of hours of sleep that afternoon before going to the police commissariat in the 7th *arrondissement* to file a report on what he had seen of the explosion on Valanis's houseboat. In the absence of any further tip-offs, he had seen no point in spending another night in Pigalle. Instead he had sent a team of policemen to comb the *quartier*, knocking on every door near the alley in which the two murders had taken place and asking questions. The chance of their learning anything of importance was remote – the inhabitants of Pigalle seldom volunteered information to the flics – but it was part of routine police procedure in cases of that kind and the director-general of the Sûreté insisted that procedure should be followed, whatever the circumstances. Sometimes, though by no means always, Gautier liked to humour him.

'There's a woman I don't know,' Madame de Saules remarked. 'The one with the dark hair and the diamond tiara.'

'She's a Russian princess,' her husband replied. 'Princesse Sophia Dashkova.'

'And how did you come to meet such an attractive creature?' his wife teased him. 'You'll be telling us she banks with you, I suppose.'

'No, but a portrait of her created a sensation at this year's Salon.'

'So that's the princess,' Michelle said. 'One cannot open a newspaper without reading about her.'

'What has she done to deserve such fame – or notoriety? I never read the papers.'

What Michelle had said was true. Since Princesse Sophia had arrived in Paris at the beginning of that season, newspapers had competed with each other in publishing highly coloured stories of her past, her loves, her fortunes and her future. Even Gautier, who took little interest in society gossip, had been unable to avoid reading some of them. Princesse Sophia was Turkish by birth, had married a wealthy Greek merchant who had conveniently died leaving her free to marry again, this time a much younger, but sickly Russian prince who had not survived long enough to give her any children. Her fortune she had inherited from the Greek, her title from the Russian. She was said to be frighteningly clever and when, after her second marriage, she had begun to study physics and mechanics, she had confounded university professors by her brilliance. The reason for her arrival in Paris was a subject for speculation. One theory was that she had been frightened into

21

leaving Russia by the recent abortive uprising, believing that it would be followed by a successful revolution, and another was that she had come as a patron of the arts to prepare the ground for visits to Paris by Russian singers and ballet dancers the following year. Some people preferred a more mundane explanation, that she had come to find a third husband.

When Michelle had finished telling these stories to Madame de Saules she said, 'They say that as a young girl she escaped from a harem and fled to Greece.'

'I won't believe that!'

'An alternative story is that her father was swindled by an unscrupulous business colleague and that she was sent to Greece to work as a nursemaid,' Monsieur de Saules told them.

'I look forward to meeting her,' Michelle said.

Before meeting the princess they spoke to several other people. At her first soirée for several months, Michelle was clearly determined to renew contacts with as many of her acquaintances as possible. For too long she had tasted the pleasures of society only vicariously, listening to the news and the gossip of women who had come to see her in her home. Now, taking Gautier with her, she toured the room, stopping only briefly to exchange words with the other guests, most of whom were known to her though not to Gautier.

Madame Mauberge's soirées differed from those of many salons in Paris in that she always invited a sprinkling of past and present Government ministers, leading politicians and important businessmen to mix with her writers, artists and musicians. One of the people whom Michelle and Gautier met that evening was Admiral Théodore Pottier. The admiral had at one time been a powerful figure in French politics, the Minister of War, and considered by many to be a likely candidate for President of the Republic. Then stories of atrocities committed by

22

the French navy in Indo-China had so outraged public opinion that Pottier had been forced to resign and his political career had never recovered from the setback. Now he had found himself a post as adviser to a firm making boating equipment, scarcely an appointment worthy of his talents and his dignity, but one has to live. He had the reputation of being a ladies' man and Gautier noticed that when he met Michelle he held on to her hand far longer and more tightly than simple politeness would have required.

When he was introduced to Gautier the admiral said, 'Inspecteur Gautier! I've heard of your reputation. People say you're uncommonly clever.'

'You're very kind, Monsieur.'

'As it happens I think you may be the very man to solve a little problem which is bothering me.'

'What problem is that?'

'We won't bore people by discussing it here. Would you be prepared to meet me at my club one day this week?'

'Willingly.'

'Then I will be in touch with you to make an appointment.'

The admiral hurried away, a sexual predator looking for women who might be susceptible to his ageing charm. Meanwhile Michelle had been gradually manoeuvring them into a position where they would be alongside Princesse Sophia Dashkova. When they reached her the princess was talking to a distant cousin of Michelle and so introductions were managed without difficulty. The princess was certainly beautiful and Gautier was surprised at her complexion which was paler and more delicate than he would have expected in anyone from the eastern Mediterranean. She appeared too young to have been married and widowed twice, not much more than thirty, Gautier supposed. The look she gave him when she was told his name was solemn and searching and he wondered whether she might be thinking it odd that a police inspector should be at a soirée where most of the other guests were drawn from the *gratin* or upper crust of Paris society. Sometimes he thought it rather strange himself.

'Our hostess is unhappy,' the princess remarked. 'The guest who was to be the principal attraction in her salon tonight has not arrived.'

'Surely that must be you,' Michelle said.

'Me? What an idea! I was invited only for my curiosity value; to bring a touch of the exotic into a Paris drawing room.'

'If that was all our hostess wanted,' Gautier said, 'she could have invited a tiger.'

The princess smiled. 'Perhaps she has.'

'Who is to be this *vedette*? This prize guest?'

'Madame Mauberge will not say. It's to be a surprise.'

They did not have long to wait for the surprise as only a few minutes later the *vedette* of the evening arrived. A manservant announced his arrival, speaking more loudly and self-consciously than he had when intoning the names of other guests, perhaps because he was unaccustomed to ushering in a guest dressed in the robes, headdress and other accoutrements of a Turkish caliph and with a jewelled dagger in his sash.

'Mother of God!' Michelle exclaimed. 'It's Jacques Mounet!'

Jacques Mounet was one of France's most popular authors and he had achieved success in an unusual way. Although he came of a good bourgeois family, his father had died leaving his mother almost penniless and with no other prospects he had become an officer in the navy, a career for which he was physically and by temperament unsuited. In an age of colonial expansion, when all the major powers of Europe were trying to extend their territories and their influence overseas, Mounet's service in the navy had taken him all over the world; to north and west Africa, the Caribbean, Turkey, India and the Orient.

Fascinated by what he saw, he began writing articles on life in these countries and of the adventures, highly coloured and sometimes imaginary, which he experienced in them. The articles, published in newspapers and reviews, were an immediate success, enthralling Frenchmen with the glimpses they gave of exotic countries which ordinary people had never seen or were likely to see. Mounet then began writing novels which were equally successful and within a few years he was able to leave the navy, build his mother a fine house in their home town of Le Havre and make a home for himself in Paris. There his habit of appearing unexpectedly dressed in Turkish clothes and sometimes smoking a hookah delighted Parisians and multiplied the sales of his books. Now it was rumoured that he was soon to be nominated for election to the most exclusive group of writers and savants, the Académie Française.

'Léontine has done it again!' Michelle said.

'Done what again?'

'Commited a faux pas with her choice of guests for this evening. One simply cannot have Jacques Mounet and Théo Pottier in the same drawing room together.'

'Why not?' Princesse Sophia asked.

'It was the articles Jacques wrote and sent back from Indo-China describing how French sailors had massacred the natives which forced Théo to resign and ruined his political career.'

'Was it not a little unfair to blame the admiral? He cannot have been there at the time.'

'It was unfair, particularly as nothing was said in the articles of the atrocities which the Indo-Chinese committed on any French sailor who fell into their hands.'

'All this was years ago,' Gautier remarked.

'Agreed, but Théo has never forgiven him. They hate each other. Really, Léontine is so absent-minded! A few

25

weeks ago she sent an invitation to Verlaine for one of her soirées.'

Gautier smiled, for the poet Verlaine had died several years previously, in 1896. He noticed that Princesse Sophia did not appear to find the story amusing and her expression as she watched Madame Mauberge taking Mounet round the drawing room to meet her other guests was one of simmering resentment. Mounet, for his part, was clearly enjoying the ceremonial and the flattery and compliments he was receiving. When finally his hostess presented him to Princesse Sophia the flourish of his exaggerated bow over her outstretched hand might have been taken for a burlesque.

'Your Highness,' he said, 'I am enchanted that I can pay homage to your beauty at last.'

'We have met before, Monsieur.'

'Surely not? It is inconceivable that I should have forgotten so momentous an occasion.'

'We have, but I was not a princess then and you were scarcely paying me homage.'

The fine edge of sarcasm to her words appeared to disconcert Mounet and he said, 'Then it is I who must apologise, Your Highness, for my lack of gallantry as well as for my poor memory.'

'The circumstances of our meeting,' Princesse Sophia replied, 'were such that no doubt you would prefer to forget it.'

3

Next morning in his office at Sûreté headquarters, Gautier studied the dossier on the two murders in Pigalle. Although very little had so far been discovered about the stabbings, the dossier was already bulky, the volume of paper seeming to grow in inverse proportion to the information it presented. The bodies of the two victims had been found in the same alley and the stab wounds from which they had died were almost identical, but otherwise the killings appeared to have nothing in common. One of the dead men was a native of Marseille named Ardot, a petty thief and pimp who had been in trouble with the police often enough but never for violence; the other was a provincial businessman from Rouen named Sandeau, who had been ill-advised enough to go out on his own into Pigalle looking for the naughty pleasures which Paris was supposed to offer at night. Ardot had been in his twenties, lithe and active but not active enough to have escaped a few scars. Sandeau was forty-two and plump and his flaccid body was unmarked except for the one fatal knife thrust. A pocket-watch and gold chain had been found on his body, together with more than a hundred francs, showing that robbery had not been the motive for his murder.

The reports of the policemen Gautier had sent into Pigalle the previous afternoon were also in the dossier. The enquiries they had made in the bistros and cafés and shops had been fruitless. No one in the *quartier* admitted

27

to having seen anything on the nights of the two murders, nor to having heard anything, nor did they know anything about the two victims. As Gautier was finishing reading the reports his principal assistant, Surat, arrived. Surat was several years older than Gautier, a courageous and conscientious police officer, who had been passed over for promotion but remained loyal to the Sûreté and even more loyal to Gautier.

Surat had also been in Pigalle the previous evening, but not in uniform and on an unofficial assignment. Some years previously Gautier's wife Suzanne had left him to live with a policeman from the 15th *arrondissement* named Gaston. She and Gaston had bought a café in Pigalle which they had run together, and Gautier dropped in there from time to time, not because he enjoyed seeing them, but to please Suzanne who had wanted to remain friends. On occasions, the visits had been useful to him when investigating a crime in the district, for Gaston had quickly been accepted in Pigalle and knew a good deal about the local scoundrels and *voyous* and their petty misdemeanours.

Then, a few months previously, Suzanne had died in childbirth, and now Gautier never called in at the Café Soleil d'Or, for he was afraid that if they met and began talking of Suzanne, Gaston would grow maudlin and weep – he was an emotional man. Gautier had no wish to talk to anyone of Suzanne, for his memories of her, his feelings of guilt and self-reproach, were his alone. So he had asked Surat to drop in on Gaston instead.

'Well, did you learn anything in Pigalle?' he asked.

'Nothing of any practical value, patron; no names, no facts.'

'But something?' Surat, with his friendliness and un-assuming manner, had a gift for attracting confidences in casual conversation.

'It may mean nothing, but the people in the *quartier* are disturbed by the two murders.'

'Disturbed?'

'Uneasy. No one talks about them and if the subject is mentioned in a café the whole place grows silent. As for the girls, there's no doubt in my mind that they are frightened.'

'Interesting!'

In Pigalle and the area of Paris to the north of it, crime was commonplace and violence not uncommon. One pimp would steal another pimp's girl, a thief would cheat his accomplice by holding back part of the haul of a robbery, occasionally one criminal would revenge himself by informing on another. Vendettas were begun quickly and ended even more quickly, usually with a knife in a dark alley, sometimes, if a woman was involved, with vitriol flung in her face. No one interfered, no one was surprised, no one commented beyond an expressive shrug of the shoulders.

'And they are wondering when he will strike again and whose turn it will be?'

'Exactly! They believe a maniac is on the loose in the *quartier*.'

To have any further enquiries made in and around the area where the two men had been stabbed would be a waste of time, Gautier decided. The police had learnt all they would ever learn from the local inhabitants. The valise and other belongings which Monsieur Sandeau had left in the modest hotel where he had been staying had been searched without revealing anything which might explain why he had been murdered. His wife was due to arrive in Paris later that morning from Rouen to claim his body, and he told Surat to meet her at the railway station and bring her to Sûreté headquarters. If there was anything she could tell them Surat would find it out. Beyond that, all he could do was to advise the local police

29

commissariat to send out more police on patrol in Pigalle for the next few evenings. The orders would not be welcomed, for policemen were as vulnerable as ordinary citizens to a swift dagger.

After Surat had left him he found his thoughts straying from the problem of the two murders in Pigalle, murders which, he suspected, might like many killings in the Paris underworld remain unsolved. Thoughts of Suzanne had triggered off other thoughts in his mind. The previous evening, after returning from Madame Mauberge's salon, he had stayed with Michelle Le Tellier until early morning. The pleasure he found in recalling their love-making was tempered by uneasiness, for in retrospect he seemed to sense that their relationship was changing. So long as she had been in mourning, Michelle had looked forward to and enjoyed his company, her appetite for their clandestine love sharpened by the knowledge that it was supposed to be forbidden to her. Now she had emerged from her chrysalis, there was a subtle difference in what she expected from him. She wanted an escort, a male hovering attentively as she fluttered from one social occasion to the next. He sensed too a change in what she was prepared to give him. She had wider interests now and was reluctant to spare the time for the long discussions of literature and art and politics which he had so much enjoyed over dinner at her apartment when she had been in mourning. Instead she appeared to wish to use him as any woman would use a complaisant male, and if he behaved well she would reward him by allowing him to make love to her. If this were true it would not be a relationship that would appeal to him.

His speculations about their future were interrupted by the arrival of a messenger to say that he should go at once to the office of the director-general. Gautier suppressed a sigh. Courtrand, the director-general, led a leisurely life, arriving at the Sûreté late and often leaving early to prepare for the many social functions which he attended, and for this reason, perhaps, summonses to see him were always urgent and he expected his instructions, however trivial, to be executed with the greatest despatch. Gautier suspected that the reason why his presence was required upstairs was unlikely to be dramatic or even interesting.

When he reached Courtrand's office he found that three of the Sûreté's other senior inspectors were already there. Courtrand, red with excitement or indignation – one could not guess which – was waving a sheet of paper at them and when he saw Gautier arrive he waved it at him as well.

'Have you seen this?' he shouted. 'Have you any idea what it means? A reign of terror! No one will be safe!' Crossing the room he threw open one of the windows. It was a gesture Gautier had seen him make only two or three times before, a sign of anger and frustration. He went on, 'We will need every available man. All leave must be cancelled. Every police commissariat in the city must be put on the alert. I shall plan the operation myself.'

'Might we be permitted to see this document, Monsieur le Directeur?' one of the other inspectors asked.

Courtrand handed the sheet of paper to the man, who read what was written on it and then passed it to the inspector standing next to him. When the paper reached Gautier he saw that it carried a heading in crude, hand-written capital letters.

THE FIFTEEN CONDEMNED ONES

Beneath the heading was a list of names and against each name was a drawing, also crudely executed, of a playing card. Each name had a different card, chosen, as far as one could tell, at random. Gautier glanced down the list.

9♦ Louis Reison-Vernet   4♣ F. Sandeau

4♥ B. Ardot   7♦ P. Bernac

A♥ Emile Loubet   2♣ Paul Valanis

2♠ P. Villon   8♥ F. Dubois

5♣ I. Grigov   A♠ Jacques Mouret

3♥ Henri Lacaze   7♠ J. Archard

5♠ Claude Rozière   3♣ A. Fleury

2♦ L. Desmarais

Some of the names Gautier recognised. Emile Loubet was the President of the Republic, Risson-Vernet was Minister of Finance, there was a deputy named Claude Rozière and a judge named Lacaze. And Valanis and Mounet were known to him personally.

'The anarchists have returned! This is their work,' Courtrand said angrily. 'And now the bombings will start.'

He was only one of many Parisians who would have remembered uneasily the wave of terror that had swept the city in the 1890s, as anarchists tried to remedy the injustices of society by bomb attacks on judges, lawyers and policemen and, in one case, on the Chamber of Deputies. The fear aroused by twelve major explosions in Paris within two years had been exacerbated by scores of false alarms and rumours, with hoaxes adding to the confusion. Such was the general nervousness that owners of apartment buildings trying to attract new tenants would advertise as a selling point that no judges or lawyers lived in the property. Some concierges even went so far as to open their doors only to people who could give a secret password, and more than one forgetful tenant was excluded from his apartment for the night.

Matters had reached a climax when the President of the Republic, Sadi Carnot, was assassinated in 1894, though not with a bomb but a knife. A few public executions with a guillotine set up outside the prison of La Roquette in front of a huge crowd of spectators, not to mention platoons of infantry, squads of cavalry and several hundred policemen, soon tempered the enthusiasm of 'Les Anars' and there were no more bombs, but more than ten years later the fear which they had provoked remained.

'I do not believe that we should assume too readily that this is the work of anarchists, Monsieur,' Gautier told Courtrand.

'How can you say that, Gautier? The list includes a

government minister, a deputy and a judge, not to mention the President of the Republic. Who else but anarchists would wish to assassinate them?'

'Agreed, Monsieur, but why should anarchists wish to kill B. Ardot and F. Sandeau?'

'Who on earth are they?'

'Unless it is an unbelievable coincidence, they are the two men found murdered in Pigalle earlier this week; a harmless provincial businessman and a pimp.'

When Gautier reached Quai des Grands-Augustins, he found that a team of workmen was already at work on the houseboat, repairing the damage that had been done by the explosion of the previous day. Splintered wood and pieces of twisted metal stripped from the deck had been heaped on the quay and the sound of hammering reverberated across the river. He had come to the houseboat after first calling at Paul Valanis's house in Avenue du Bois where he had been told that the Greek would be spending the morning putting in hand the repairs to the vessel.

He was looking for Valanis on the instructions of Courtrand. The director-general had decided that as many as possible of the people named in the anonymous document which he had received that morning should be warned that an attempt might be made on their lives. Including the President of the Republic, six were prominent people in one sphere of life or another, two were already dead and the remaining seven were names that were not known either to Courtrand or to any of the senior inspectors. Courtrand had also decided that it was appropriate that he should warn the President personally, and had asked for an audience. He had then gone home to change into his best frock coat, leaving his senior inspectors to divide the other five prominent names up between themselves and to begin inquiries that might identify the remaining seven names on the list. Because he knew both Valanis and Mounet, Gautier had agreed to go and speak to them.

When he reached the houseboat, he saw that there was a man standing guard alongside the gangplank. Although he wore a sailor's uniform, the man did not have the weather-beaten complexion of one who spent his life at sea. His face had the pallor associated more often with late nights in ill-ventilated cabarets and bistros and his physique was intimidating. When Gautier explained the reason for his visit, the man shouted to another sailor on deck that a flic had arrived to see the patron. The sailor went below and returned presently to say that the patron would see the inspector.

Valanis was in the owner's stateroom, a room furnished in nautical style with charts on the walls, chronometers and compasses which, Gautier suspected, played no part in the navigation of the vessel. He and another man were studying a set of engineer's drawings that had been spread out on the table.

'I can give you five minutes, Gautier,' he said. 'What is it that you want this time?'

'To warn you, Monsieur.'

'Warn me? What am I supposed to have done?'

'You misunderstand me. This warning is for your benefit. I have to tell you that your name is on a list of people which has been sent anonymously to the Sûreté. The implication is that all those on the list are to be assassinated.'

Valanis made a small, contemptuous noise. 'The work of some lunatic, I suppose.'

'Possibly, but two men whose names are on the list have already been murdered.'

What Gautier had told him did not appear to disconcert Valanis in any way. Although short in stature he was powerfully built, and a man who had spent his life on the edge of crime, trafficking in drugs and women and arms, would be accustomed to danger. In Paris he had adopted

the dress and manners of society, wearing only silk shirts
and handmade boots, having his nails manicured and his
black hair plastered down with brilliantine, but one sensed
that this was no more than a veneer and that the ruthless-
ness and aggression which had helped him to survive and
grow wealthy were never far below the surface.

'Can you think of anyone who might wish you harm?'
Gautier asked him.

'Several people. In my business one makes many
enemies.'

'The police will endeavour to give you whatever protection we can, but with so many people under threat it will
not be easy.'

'You need take no special measures on my behalf. I
have the means to take care of myself.'

'But you were unable to prevent your boat being
blown up.'

Gautier had heard officially that morning that the explosion on the houseboat had been caused by a home-made
but effective bomb.

'The bomb cannot have been meant to kill Monsieur
Valanis,' said the man who was standing next to him at
his desk. 'Everyone knows that he never sleeps on board
when the boat is in Paris.'

'No, and when I discover who was responsible he will
suffer,' Valanis said viciously. 'He has forced me to post-
pone our cruise for a week.'

'More than a week, I'm afraid, Monsieur.'

'A week should give you plenty of time to finish the
repairs. Employ all the men you need. Rig up lamps on
deck so they can work all night.'

Gautier had heard about the cruises which Valanis made
from time to time in his boat. The names of his guests,
the places they would visit and the entertainment which
their host would provide for them were all reported with a
wealth of detail in the society columns of the newspapers.

Almost always one of the guests would be a lady whose name was then being linked with that of Valanis. Newspapers even hinted that the main purpose of a cruise was to entice the lady into a situation where she could most easily be seduced, away from the prying eyes of her neighbours, her relatives, even of her husband.

'Monsieur Mounet is a ship-builder,' Valanis explained to Gautier.

'A boat-builder would be a more accurate description,' Mounet said. 'Years ago our family built ships. Now we make our living by designing and constructing pleasure vessels, yachts mainly.'

'In Paris?'

'No, Le Havre, but I am frequently in Paris. Most of our clients are wealthy Parisians or the English. And when Monsieur Valanis telegraphed me telling me of the damage to his boat I came at once to see what could be done.'

'Are you by any chance related to Jacques Mounet the author? I understand he comes from Le Havre too.'

'Yes. We are cousins.'

'The five minutes which I agreed to give you are over, Gautier,' Valanis said. He had no interest in Mounet's background. 'We cannot waste any more time on this nonsense. You can assure your superiors that I have made a note of their warning. Now Monsieur Mounet has work to do.'

Up on deck Gautier noticed that one of the crew was repainting the name on the bows of the houseboat. The former name he recalled had been 'DESIREE'. That had been obliterated and a new name, 'ANTOINETTE', was being painted over it. The man who had been standing guard at the gangplank was no longer there and his place had been taken by a smaller, more likely-looking sailor. Gautier stopped to speak to the man. He was inclined to agree with Pierre Mounet that the bomb could not have been intended to kill Valanis.

'I was desolate when I heard that two of your shipmates had been killed by that bomb.'

'Yes. One of them was a chum of mine.'

'What was his name, may I ask?'

'Bernac. Pierre Bernac.'

'And the other man who was killed?'

'Villon. Also Pierre. He was the unlucky one for he was only sleeping on board to do his friend Collet a good turn. Collet had gone to a family wedding in Calais.'

'So I have heard. Poor devil!' Gautier commented. Then he added, 'We'll find out who placed that bomb in the ship. You can be sure of that.'

'I hope so. I want to watch the guillotine fall on the swine's neck.'

'Tell me, have you or any other member of the crew seen any suspicious characters lurking around on the quay near your boat recently?'

The sailor shook his head. 'Not as far as I know.'

'So you've no idea who might have put the bomb on the boat?'

'No, but we did have some trouble with a man here the other day.'

'What kind of trouble?'

'He arrived and demanded to go on board and see the owner. When we told him that Monsieur Valanis was not here he wanted to search the boat; said some property of his had been stolen and that it might be hidden on board.'

'What did you do?'

'We wouldn't let him on board of course and when he tried to force his way across the gangplank we threw him off. He got in a terrible rage, cursed and swore at us, said he would be back.'

'Do you know who the man was?'

'Oh yes. He showed me his visiting card when he first arrived. A funny name it was. The Great Astrux.'

4

Jacques Mounet lived in rue Murillo near Parc Monceau, a part of Paris which was rapidly becoming the most fashionable place for wealthy bourgeois families. His apartment was large enough for him to be able to indulge his fantasies and arrange a series of rooms in different styles which would remind him of the exotic places that he had visited and which he had described so colourfully in his novels and articles: Turkey, Arabia, Persia and Indo-China.

He received Gautier that morning in the Turkish room, seated on a silk divan and smoking his hookah. The room had an elaborate carved ceiling in crimson and gold, sumptuous wall hangings, thick Armenian rugs, coffee tables in cedarwood inlaid with ivory and silver lamps. Standing on an easel was a portrait in oils of a strikingly lovely woman who by her colouring and dress must also be from Turkey. Mounet was dressed not in Turkish dress but in the rough vestments of a bedouin from the desert.

'What can I do for you, Inspecteur?' Although they had been introduced at Madame Mauberge's soirée, Mounet clearly did not remember Gautier. 'Are you going to tell me that there has been another complaint against me?'

'A complaint, Monsieur?'

'My neighbours in the building complain to the police from time to time. They dislike the smell of incense and other aromatic substances which I burn in this apartment. Foolish of them really, because the smoke and smells of these substances and of the herbs and spices which my

39

cook uses when preparing my food are beneficial to the health and give protection against disease.'

'The reason for my visit is not a complaint. On the contrary, I hope that when you hear what I have to say, you will be glad that I came.'

Gautier told him of the list of 'Condemned Ones', how it had reached the Sûreté and that four of the men named on the list were already dead. Mounet's reaction was very different from the sang-froid of Valanis. Even before Gautier had finished he had jumped up from the divan, thrust his hookah on one side and begun walking up and down the room. His agitation was painful to watch.

'Who else is on this list?' he demanded.

'I am not at liberty to tell you the names, Monsieur.'

Courtrand had decided that to publish the full list would cause unnecessary panic and that no one should be told of its existence except the people whose names were on it and the Prefect of Police.

'What possible reason could anyone have for wishing to kill so many people? What do the intended victims have in common?'

'We are looking at each name, speaking to as many of the people as we can identify, to find out if there is a link. In your case can you think of anyone who hates you enough to wish you dead?'

'Many people. My dear Gautier, any author of integrity makes enemies. Whenever I come across hypocrisy or incompetence I never hesitate to expose it. Cardinals and cabinet ministers, princes and poets, fortune hunters and philanderers, they have all felt the lash of my pen and I've no doubt they hate me for it.'

'Would you care to give me any names, Monsieur?'

Mounet shook his head. 'Not at this stage, Inspecteur. I would not wish to throw suspicion on anyone who did not deserve it. Most of the incidents I am describing took place weeks or even months ago and the desire for revenge

40

softens with time. I will review the matter and let you know if there is anything useful I can tell you.'

'The Sûreté is working out a plan to give you and the others on this infamous list as much protection as possible. In the meantime, Monsieur, please be circumspect.'

Mounet's alarm appeared to have abated and Gautier decided that there was nothing to be gained by prolonging his visit, but before he could take his leave a servant came into the room carrying a tray with a silver coffee pot of oriental design and two cups. Like Mounet, the servant was wearing a costume which Gautier assumed to be typical of some Middle Eastern country. He was a handsome man of about thirty, well built, and one had the impression that he was ill-at-ease both in the long plain robe and skullcap and sandals and in the role of servant.

'Bravo Yussif,' Mounet said cheerily, 'as always you have timed your arrival perfectly. You'll take coffee, Inspecteur?'

After Yussif had left the room and they were sipping their coffee, Gautier remarked, 'Did you find your man in Turkey, Monsieur?'

Mounet laughed. 'You might be excused for thinking that, but no. It's a harmless little deception which we both enjoy. Yussif is really Lucien and he was born in Brittany. He was a shipmate of mine.'

'In the navy?'

'Yes. He was a rating and I befriended him when I learnt he was an orphan. He is devoted to me.'

For lack of anything better to say, Gautier told Mounet that he had met his cousin that morning. 'Pierre?' Mounet said. 'He's in Paris then. I wonder what brings him here.'

'He's supervising repairs to the houseboat which was damaged by a bomb yesterday morning. You may have heard about it.'

'Of course. Pierre built that boat for Valanis.'

While they had been speaking Gautier found himself glancing at the portrait on its easel which stood directly in his line of vision. Mounet must have noticed the glances for he smiled.

'Do you admire that painting, Inspecteur?'

'Very much.'

'It was painted here in Paris by a well-known artist who worked entirely from pencil sketches which I made of the lady and brought home with me from Constantinople.'

'Then the lady is Turkish, I presume.'

'Have you ever read any of my novels, Inspecteur?'

'I am ashamed to say no.'

'Then you must be almost the only person who hasn't. Try reading *Seraglio*. Many people think it was my best novel and it will tell you the story of the girl in the portrait.'

When he left rue Murillo, Gautier found a *fiacre* to drive him to the Ile de la Cité. On the way he stopped by the row of *bouquinistes* who had their stalls along the banks of the Seine. Jacques Mounet had probably been right when he said that most people in Paris had read his books, but evidently they were not books which were kept to be read again, for Gautier found several second-hand copies of *Seraglio* from which to choose. He bought the least dog-eared he could find and paid only a few sous for it. On the same stall he saw a pack of playing cards and on an impulse bought it as well.

He had not yet lunched so he went to a café in place Dauphine, a small tree-lined square behind the Palais de Justice. At one time the café had been owned by a widow from Normandy and her daughter Janine who, for a time, had been Gautier's mistress. They had sold the place and moved back to Normandy but he still ate there from time to time, usually in the evenings, even though he had never become friendly with the new proprietor and did not greatly care for his style of cuisine. That proved, he often told himself, that he had become a creature of habit and, like many men who lived alone, lazy as well.

As he ate the café's *plat du jour* of pork and lentils, he flicked quickly through Mounet's book. *Seraglio* was the story of a French naval officer whose ship had been sent to Turkey in the late 1870s as part of an allied fleet of warships from the major powers of Europe, ostensibly to show their displeasure at the Turks' persecution of Christian minorities. Although the book was a romance, Mounet had taken the opportunity in the first pages to attack the French Government for its hypocrisy. The real reason for the expedition, he claimed, had been to explore the possibility of acquiring colonies for France in the Middle East. His accusations and the scorn with which he made them could scarcely have pleased the Government of the day and Gautier wondered whether, as a serving officer, Mounet might not have been disciplined for his impertinence.

After he had eaten he put the novel aside to read later, and as he finished his demi-carafe of wine he opened the pack of cards and spread them out on the table. He was intrigued by the fact that whoever had composed the list of the Fifteen Condemned Ones should have drawn a picture of a playing card against each of the names. This must have some significance, he assumed, and, picking out from the pack the fifteen cards that had been drawn on the list, he laid them side by side in front of him. As far as he could see there was no obvious connection between the people on the list and either the denomination or the suit of the cards against their names. All he did notice was that no picture cards had been drawn, nor any card higher than a nine. He wondered why. Then he checked his copy of the list of Condemned Ones to see what cards had been used for the four people who were already dead. Ardot had the four of hearts against his name and Sandeau the four of clubs, while the two sailors, Villon and Bernac, had been represented by the two of spades and the seven of diamonds respectively.

Evidently the intended victims were not being murdered in the order in which they had been named on the list, so he took the four cards of the dead men and separated them from the other eleven. He could find no mathematical sequence in them, even when he changed the order of them around into every possible combination. Checking his list again he saw that President Loubet had the ace of hearts against his name and Jacques Mounet the ace of spades against his. Was that meant to signify that the president was the heart of the country? Fortune-tellers, he had been told, took the ace of spades as symbolising death. Mounet might be regarded as associated with death because he had been an officer in a French warship, but the connection seemed tenuous to say the least. He shook his head, conscious that his speculations were getting him nowhere.

He was picking up all the cards on the table and rearranging them in suits, when he heard what he thought was a single clap of thunder followed by its rumbling echo. No more claps followed and when he glanced out of the window of the café he saw that the day was still fine, with a watery sunshine slanting through the trees of place Dauphine. As he picked up the cards he reflected that, apart from those that were already dead, all the people on the list of Condemned Ones who were known to the Sûreté would by then have been warned that their lives might be in danger. The remaining five presented a problem and he supposed he should begin to tackle it and attempt to identify the people. Checking with his copy of the list he studied the names.

Archard   Desmarais   Dubois   Grigov   Fleury

He recalled Michelle Le Tellier telling him of a Russian singer named Grigov who she said would be appearing at the Paris Opéra later that season, and for a start he might

44

check and find out whether he was in the city. He had put away the cards and was paying the wife of the café owner what he owed her when Surat arrived from Sûreté headquarters.

'Patron! I hoped I might find you here.'

'Why? What has happened?'

'A bomb has exploded in the Palais de Justice. Didn't you hear it?'

5

The explosion in the Palais de Justice had killed no one, and only one man, an usher, had been slightly injured by flying fragments of glass as he was walking along a nearby corridor. The bomb had been placed in one of the smaller courts where a case of fraud was being tried, but it had exploded after the trial had been adjourned for lunch and the court was empty. An hour or so earlier, counting the judges, lawyers for the prosecution and defence, witnesses and court officials, there would have been at least forty people present. Those who had been there then would no doubt consider that they had a lucky escape, but in the light of past experience it was not surprising that the explosion had been mistimed. Home-made bombs were notoriously unreliable and several made by anarchists a few years earlier had exploded at the wrong time or not at all. In more than one case they had killed the men who had been placing them.

When he learnt that Judge Lacaze, whose name he remembered was on the list of Condemned Ones, had been presiding in the court where the bomb had exploded, Gautier went to Sûreté headquarters, expecting that the director-general would wish to hold another conference to discuss the incident and to issue fresh instructions to his inspectors. Courtrand, however, had not returned from a lunch which was being held that day in the Hôtel de Ville in honour of a visiting delegation from the Municipality of Brussels.

Deciding that he could not wait for Courtrand's return, Gautier sent a team of policemen to the Palais de

Justice where they were to make intensive enquiries, asking everyone who had been in the vicinity of the court where the bomb had exploded whether they had seen anyone carrying a package or otherwise behaving in a suspicious manner. There were other enquiries which he intended to make himself, but first he went to the Palais de Justice and consulted the archives where one could find a complete report of all cases that had been tried in the courts. It did not take long to establish that Judge Lacaze had also presided at the trial two years previously when Astrux had been found guilty of criminal libel.

From the newspaper's offices Gautier went to rue La Boétie, where Astrux lived and where he had what he chose to describe as his consulting rooms. The manservant who let Gautier in made him wait in an ante-room, telling him that the master was engaged with a client. After ten minutes or so the client, whom Gautier recognised as a well-known impresario, owner of two music halls and one of the largest café-concerts in Paris, came out from the consulting room and Gautier was admitted.

Astrux was a tall man with a handsome face that looked as though it had been sculpted in very pale marble. He wore his hair long, and that, with his untidy grey beard and distant expression of a visionary, gave the impression that he was a prophet just in from the wilderness. The curtains of the room were drawn, giving it an appropriate atmosphere of mystery, and Astrux was wearing a long scarlet robe embroidered with symbols which one supposed must have an occult or supernatural significance. The signs of the zodiac were painted on the ceiling and in one corner of the room there was a model of the universe with planets suspended around a giant sun.

'Since you did not make an appointment to see me, I assume that you are not requiring my professional services, Inspecteur.' Astrux's voice was deep and resonant.

47

'No, Monsieur. I am here in connection with a disturbance which you are alleged to have created at a houseboat on the Seine recently.'

'Surely they have not had the impertinence to make a complaint,' Astrux said indignantly. 'It is I who should be complaining.'

'Why is that?'

'Were you not told that I only went to the boat to reclaim property which had been stolen from me? From this apartment?'

'What property, Monsieur?'

'A diamond and ruby necklace. Valanis sent two of his sailors here and in my absence they forced their way into the apartment, threatened my servants and when they found the necklace took it away with them.'

'Have you reported the theft to the police?'

'How could I? A young lady of good family is involved.' Astrux paused and Gautier wondered whether that was all he was prepared to say or whether he was elaborating a suitable story to explain why he had a necklace. Finally he went on reluctantly. 'For some months now this young lady has been visiting me for consultations; secretly, because her relatives do not approve. She has no money of her own and so she gave me the necklace as payment for my fees.'

The story was plausible. Ladies in Paris society consulted astrologers and clairvoyants and went to have their palms read by fortune-tellers as readily as they sought the advice of fashionable physicians on their petty ailments, and a young woman with no income of her own might well have difficulty in paying the exorbitant fees which Astrux would charge for giving her a glimpse into her future.

'Then why did Monsieur Valanis think he was entitled to take the necklace?'

'He claims it was he who gave it to the young lady and that it cost several hundred thousand francs.'

'Do you think it did?'

'I did not have it valued. You must understand, Inspecteur, that I intended to give the necklace back to the young lady just as soon as she could find the money to pay what she owed me.'

This time Gautier was not inclined to believe Astrux. He knew that the man lived well in a large apartment with several servants and entertained in style. Recently the newspapers had reported that at the last Salon de l'automobile he had bought the latest and most expensive De Dion Bouton. People did not earn and spend money on that scale without having a good understanding of its value.

'May I ask, Monsieur, where you were in the early hours of yesterday morning?'

'How early? Or should it be how late?'

'Let us say about five o'clock.'

'In bed of course. I am not one of those debauched clubmen who spend their nights in dissipation and return home only at dawn.'

'Does anyone else sleep in the apartment?' Gautier knew that Astrux was unmarried.

'My servants do. Some in the apartment itself and others in rooms on the top floor of the building where servants from other families also sleep.' Astrux was about to say something more about his domestic arrangements when he checked himself. He stared at Gautier, incredulously at first and then with growing indignation. 'God in Heaven! Now I see the point of these questions! You believe I may have placed that bomb on Valanis's houseboat. I read about the explosion in the newspapers!'

'And did you, Monsieur?'

'Do you think I am a criminal? An anarchist?'

'You have a reason for wishing to revenge yourself on Monsieur Valanis.'

'You cannot be serious, Inspecteur! What do I know of bombs? Where would I get one?' Astrux's voice, which

49

usually had a deep resonance calculated to impress his clients, had moved up in pitch. Gautier wondered whether this was just through indignation or whether fear might also be a factor. 'And why have you chosen me as the most likely suspect?'

'I know of no one else who has a reason for wishing to harm the gentleman.'

'Do you not? I could name you plenty – businessmen he has swindled, wronged husbands, fathers of girls he has seduced.'

Gautier decided he would not press Astrux for names. He had come to question him on an impulse, more through curiosity than with any expectation of learning the truth about the explosion on the houseboat, and curiosity alone, as he knew from experience, seldom solved crimes. Patience, much hard work and the kind of imagination that guides intuitive thinking would all be needed before the person or people behind the bizarre threat of fifteen murders could be discovered. If he and his colleagues at the Sûreté were fortunate they might learn the answer in time to save at least some of the lives in danger. So he thanked Astrux for seeing him and prepared to leave.

'I cannot pretend that your visit was welcome,' Astrux said coldly. He appeared to have recovered both his composure and his voice. 'My profession is an exacting one and my skills require a high degree of concentration. Outside in the waiting room you will find a lady who has come to consult me. Perhaps you would be kind enough to ask her to wait till I send for her. I shall need time to compose myself before I am in a mood to communicate with the powers that guide me.'

There was someone waiting in the anteroom, but at first Gautier thought that Astrux had been mistaken and that it was not a woman. It was, however, and she was wearing a man's suit and derby hat. He looked at her more closely and realised that she was Princesse Sophia Dashkova. She smiled, recognising him at once, and he went to kiss her hand.

'I did not expect to find you here, Monsieur Gautier. Don't tell me that you need the help of the Great Astrux to solve your crimes!'

'Alas, no, Madame. We poor policemen cannot afford the services of the supernatural. We must rely on our own dull wits.'

'From what I've heard, yours are anything but dull. What did Astrux foretell for your future then?' She was mocking him, but not unkindly.

'An unexpected meeting with a beautiful woman of mystery.'

'A romantic meeting?'

'He said that only time will tell.'

'You're incorrigible! And did he not predict marriage for you?'

'Marriage? That would be most unlikely.'

'That isn't what I have heard. They say that a certain lady has designs in that direction.' Gautier only smiled, so the princess continued. 'What else did Astrux say?'

'He asked if you would mind waiting for a few minutes until he can re-establish a rapport with his unseen friends.'

'I am happy to wait provided you will wait with me.' She patted the chair next to hers and as Gautier sat down she looked at him thoughtfully, as though she had a plan in mind. 'What will you do when you leave here, Monsieur?'

'I must go to headquarters and write a report. After that I will come off duty.'

'Why don't you call and see me after you leave the Sûreté? My apartment is only just across the river in Faubourg St Germain.'

'With the greatest pleasure, Madame,' Gautier agreed, although he had no idea why he was being invited to call on the princess.

51

'Could you be there by, say, seven o'clock?'

'Easily.'

'Excellent!'

While they were talking Astrux came in from the room in which he gave his consultations, crossed to the princess and took both her hands in his in what one assumed was a gesture of homage. Then, bowing his head, he intoned a few words in a strange language, in the manner of a priest pronouncing a blessing. He appeared disconcerted to find that Gautier was still there and glanced at him suspiciously, wondering perhaps what he might have been saying to the princess.

'Come, Your Highness. I can tell from celestial signs that today is a propitious day for us to look into your future.'

In his office at Sûreté headquarters Gautier wrote a brief report on his interviews with Valanis and Jacques Mounet, describing how each of them had reacted to the news that their lives might be in danger. He did not mention his visit to Astrux's consulting rooms.

As he wrote the report he found his attention wandering. He recalled his conversation with Princesse Sophia in Astrux's apartment. She had said that a lady had him in mind as a possible husband and he wondered whether the remark had been no more than a light-hearted tease, the kind of remark a woman might make to any man whom she knew to be a widower, or whether it was based on gossip she had heard. Since his wife Suzanne had died he had once or twice formed the impression that Michelle Le Tellier might be thinking that they might marry, but he had always dismissed the idea. Michelle came of a good family and was considered to have married beneath her when she chose Jacques Le Tellier, an editor of a modest newspaper.

She had once told him of a remark which an elderly uncle of hers had made when he heard she was marrying for love. A week of ecstacy in bed, he had said acidly, and a lifetime at the wrong end of the dinner table. As a husband Le Tellier had not been conspicuous as a provider, nor for devotion or fidelity, and Gautier could not believe that Michelle would risk making the same mistake for a second time.

When he finished the report and had taken it to Courtrand's office, where it would be waiting for him the next morning, it was approaching seven o'clock, so he found a *fiacre* to drive him to rue Jacob where the princess had rented a small house. The manservant who opened the door led him directly to the drawing room where Princesse Sophia was waiting, but she was not alone. Her other visitor was Admiral Pottier.

'Monsieur Gautier!' The princess exclaimed. 'You're early!'

'Am I, Madame?' Gautier had found that it seldom paid to contradict a woman.

'I told the admiral you had asked to see me on police business but I was expecting you later.'

'Would you like me to withdraw and return another time?'

'No, no, not now you're here,' the princess said quickly. 'The admiral will forgive us, I'm sure.'

Admiral Pottier's expression was anything but forgiving. He gave a grunt which might just conceivably have been intended as assent. The three of them chatted for a while, the polite small talk of a Paris drawing room.

'The admiral and I have the greatest of all bonds,' the princess said, 'a common hatred.'

'Who is the unfortunate person?'

'That scoundrel Jacques Mounet,' Pottier replied.

'Why should you hate Monsieur Mounet, Madame?'

'Because of the wrong he has done my country. The picture he painted of Turkey in his novel was a travesty of the truth. He only wanted to titillate and shock his readers so the book would sell. And now he mocks us by aping our dress and our manners.'

'And he was a disgrace to our navy.'

'For what he wrote about Indo-China?'

'Not only for that. He did not behave like an officer. Do you know he had close friendships with the ratings. One of his commanding officers had strong suspicions that he was a homosexual. No, he should have been courtmartialled and cashiered as I wanted. That would have been the end of him and his writing.'

Gautier remembered little of the sensation that Mounet's articles had aroused, so he said nothing. In any event, neither the princess nor Pottier seemed inclined to say any more about Mounet. So to change the subject he said to Pottier, 'Yesterday you told me you wished to see me in connection with some problem. Would you care to arrange a date and time now?'

'I cannot recall saying that I wished to see you.'

'Yes, Admiral. At Madame Mauberge's soirée.'

'You must be mistaken. I have no problems,' Pottier replied. He appeared embarrassed at being reminded of what he had said the previous evening and, perhaps to hide his confusion, he took his leave of the princess with no more than the barest pretence of courtesy and left them abruptly. When they were alone the princess smiled at Gautier.

'I owe you an apology, Monsieur.'

Gautier smiled back. 'Why? Because you invited me here so that you could rid yourself of Admiral Pottier?'

'Yes, I admit it. Last evening when he overheard me say to someone that I had no engagements tonight, he insisted that he should call on me. If you had not arrived I believe he would have stayed until I would have been forced to invite him to dinner.'

'That's unforgivable! Has the man no manners?'

'He was very importunate and was beginning to make indelicate proposals when you arrived. So I am in your debt, but I used you shamefully.'

'I am delighted to have been of service, Madame.' Gautier stood up. 'And now I shall leave you to dine in peace.'

'No, don't leave. Stay at least to have an aperitif.'

'Are you sure I will not be imposing on you?'

'Not at all! Stay, but first let me go and change out of these ridiculous clothes.' She laughed. 'I put them on hoping that a display of masculinity might cool the admiral's ardour, but the little stratagem failed. I won't be long and while you're waiting my maid will bring you an aperitif.'

Hearing her reason for dressing in men's clothes re-assured Gautier. Like everyone else in Paris he had heard stories of a growing cult of lesbianism among a group of women, mainly writers and artists, together with a few wealthy women from society. Missy, the youngest daughter of the Duc de Morny, was the leader of the clique and she found a willing disciple in Colette, the novelist, who for a while went everywhere wearing a bracelet inscribed with the words 'I belong to Missy'. Another leading lesbian was Winnaretta Singer, daughter of the American sewing-machine millionaire and now the widow of Prince Edmond de Polignac. When he saw Princesse Sophia wearing men's clothes, Gautier had wondered whether she too might have sapphic inclinations, especially since Nathalie Clifford Barney, the most determined and unabashed among the lesbians of Paris, had an apartment at 20 rue Jacob, only a few doors from the princess's house.

While he was waiting, the princess's maid came into the drawing room with a decanter of port and small Venetian glasses on a tray. Gautier did not care much for port, finding its sweetness too cloying, and preferred the bitter, herbal taste of some of the many French aperitifs, but he let the the maid pour him a glass and chatted to her as she did so.

Her name, she told him, was Marie-Ann and she was an extraordinarily pretty girl with eyes which, most Frenchmen would remark, were by no means cold. The position of personal maid to an attractive woman living alone like the princess was one coveted by young, ambitious girls. They might expect not only to be given their mistress's expensive clothes after she had finished with them and to receive generous *pourboires* from her admirers, but very often they might attract the attention of a man wealthy enough to set them up in an apartment of their own, from where they could start a profitable career as a cocotte. Some of the best-known courtesans of the day, 'the great horizontals' as they were cynically called, had started in that way.

When Princesse Sophia returned she was dressed more conventionally, but also conservatively, not in the bright colours which were then the fashion for evening wear. She poured herself a glass of port and sat down opposite Gautier.

'How did you enjoy your consultation with Astrux this morning?' he asked her.

'Why do you ask? Do I sense that you do not approve of him?'

'Frankly, Madame, I did not believe that an intelligent woman like you would take him seriously.'

'I don't, nor do I believe in astrology or magic or the supernatural. I went to see Monsieur Astrux with a business proposition.'

'And did he accept?'

'Willingly. For him the future is strictly a saleable commodity.'

'You intrigue me.'

'I shall tell you, but in confidence.'

'You can rely on me not to repeat what you say.'

The princess told him that the following year she would be bringing an opera company with supporting ballet dancers to Paris. Astrux wrote a column every week for a leading newspaper in which he made predictions of what would shortly happen in the political and social world. The proposal the princess had put to him was that before next year's season began he should predict an outstanding success for the tour she was arranging and mention it and its leading performers whenever he could.

'Is this a common practice in the theatre?'

'I don't know whether anyone has had the idea before, but if they had it would be in America. There they go to any lengths to get favourable mentions in newspapers for actresses or music-hall performers. They call it "publicity". The schemes that were devised to get publicity for Sarah Bernhardt when she toured America in 1880 were past belief. They even bought her a crocodile and made her take it everywhere with her until the poor beast died of a surfeit of champagne.'

'But what you are planning will deceive the public.' Gautier hoped that his remark would not sound too censorious.

'Not at all! My opera company will be a success. And anyway it is the only defence we have against the critics. A critic can destroy any production however excellent merely on a whim. Many of them write their reviews after seeing only the first act.' Gautier made no comment, so she added, 'It is most important for me that next year's visit to Paris should be a success.'

'Important financially?'

'No. The amount of money involved is really trifling. It is important for my reputation.' The princess sighed. 'Often I wish that I had never become interested in opera.'

She was silent for a while, as though she were brooding over the mistake she had made in becoming involved in opera. Gautier decided it might be an opportune time to

57

leave, but when he suggested it she said, 'Why? Do you have to go?'

'No,' he replied and added, joking, 'If I stay much longer I may force you to invite me to dinner.'

'There is no danger of that. My cook is ill and I was planning to manage on a bowl of soup.' She looked at him. 'There is an alternative, though.'

'Madame?'

'You could take me to dinner.'

'It would give me the greatest pleasure.'

'But not to anywhere chic, please. I am weary of the Ritz and Maxim's and Lucas. What I have not yet done and would very much like would be to eat in a good bourgeois restaurant; a place to which an ordinary Frenchman would take his family. Do you know of one?'

'Several.'

A restaurant which matched the description she had given him was La Bouchée d'Or in rue Vivienne. Suzanne's father would take the two of them there, together with his wife, their other daughter and her husband, whenever they had an occasion for a modest family celebration. Gautier and Princesse Sophia drove there in a *fiacre* and when they arrived he saw that the place had not changed. The patron still presided in the kitchen while his wife sat at a desk making out the bills and collecting the money. Even the waiters in their long white aprons were the same men as he remembered.

'I feel more at home here than any of the restaurants where one finds *tout Paris*,' Princesse Sophia said looking round the room after they had ordered their meal. 'You and I come from the same background, Jean-Paul, good bourgeois stock. My father was a merchant. What was yours?'

'A civil servant. He worked in the department of tax collection.'

'Ah! So you have a guilty secret!'

'Yes. Please don't tell my friends I'm a tax collector's son!'

'People laugh at the *petits fonctionnaires*, but they are the backbone of the country.'

'And you? Have you a secret also? Is it true that you escaped from a harem?'

She laughed. 'What a story! The truth is much less romantic.'

The truth she told him was that her father, who had a small but profitable business selling saddles, harnesses and high quality leather goods, had been ruined after being persuaded to invest in a speculative deal involving contraband. Sophia, then sixteen, had been betrothed to a man much older than herself whom she found repugnant, and to escape marrying him she had fled to Greece, where she found a position as a children's nursemaid in a Greek family. Within two years she had married a widower, a wealthy man, who had died before she was twenty-four, leaving her a substantial income. With no ties in Greece and unwilling to return to Turkey, she had travelled through Serbia, Montenegro, Italy, Switzerland, Austria and Germany. Then, in Baden–Baden, she had met a young, impoverished and sickly Russian prince. Their honeymoon and marriage, she told Gautier, had been ecstatic but shortlived, and in less than three years, even though she had taken him to a sanatorium in Switzerland and nursed him herself, the prince had died of consumption.

'And so I am left alone again.' The princess looked at Gautier mischievously as she added, 'And in need of police protection.'

'From Admiral Pottier? Perhaps he has ambitions to become your third husband.'

'What! The man must be nearly thirty years older than I!'

'But he is unattached. His wife died some years ago.'

Princesse Sophia snorted scornfully. One could see that she was enjoying her meal. She ate hungrily and without any of the affectations which society had deemed to be an essential part of good manners. The ordinary *vin du pays* which Gautier had ordered also met with her approval, for its full flavour, she told him, reminded her of the wine back home. After dinner she smoked a cigarette, a defiance of convention, for although a few daring women were beginning to smoke, none of them would have done so in public.

'Tell me, Jean-Paul.' It was the second time she had used his christian name, another breach of convention, and Gautier wondered how she had come to know it. 'What case are you working on at the present time?'

'The matter of that bomb which exploded on a houseboat in the Seine the other day. No doubt you have heard about it.'

'Yes. I may have even heard the bomb itself. Something wakened me early that morning.'

'The houseboat belongs to a countryman of yours, Paul Valanis. Do you know him?'

'I know of him. They say he's very wealthy.'

'He is, and unscrupulous.'

The princess seemed to find no interest in Valanis or his houseboat. She said, 'Men like Théodore Pottier amaze me.'

'Why is that?'

'He's a shameless womaniser himself, but insanely jealous of the women in his family.'

'He has daughters?'

'And a granddaughter. They say that twenty years ago he seriously wounded a man in a duel, defending the honour of one of his daughters.'

'That must have damaged his career.' Although duelling was against the law, the authorities chose to ignore the many duels that were fought secretly in the Bois de Boulogne, provided that neither of the adversaries was killed or seriously wounded. Honour was satisfied with a scratch from the blade of an épée, and even when both pistol shots missed.

'It was hushed up. In those days the admiral had powerful friends. Now he's in a frenzy of rage because some man, a womaniser like himself, is trying to seduce his granddaughter.'

'What's her name?'

'Antoinette.'

6

Next morning Gautier did what he had never done before in his office at Sûreté headquarters; he read a novel. He had begun the book the previous evening when he had returned home after dining with Princesse Sophia Dashkova and continued reading into the early hours of the morning. *Seraglio* was not the kind of story that appealed to him, for he found it too sentimental and contrived, but Mounet's descriptions of life in Turkey were vibrant and vivid, even if they were not, as Princesse Sophia had suggested, scrupulously accurate. Gautier was a rapid reader and had finished two-thirds of the book before putting it down. Now, as he waited for the director-general to arrive and give fresh instructions to the inspectors who were working on the affair of the Condemned Ones, he had time to finish it.

The novel told the story of a French naval officer whose ship, together with those of other European powers, had been sent to Turkish waters as a gesture of displeasure at the persecution by the Turks of Christian minorities in their country. The young officer had contrived to spend a good deal of time on shore and one day, looking through a window, he had caught a glimpse of a young girl and was so obsessed by her beauty that he was determined to become her lover. Since she was one of the wives in the harem of a wealthy and powerful Turk, this was an extremely difficult and dangerous ambition. He taught himself Turkish, rented a house and hired a young Turk as his servant. Eventually, through the cunning and resourcefulness of the Turk and with the aid of liberal bribes, a meeting was arranged. Yasmine, for this was the name Mounet had given the girl, immediately fell in love with the French officer and from then on they met as often as they could, Yasmine being smuggled out of the harem whenever her husband was away on business. The novel was spiced with titillating descriptions of their love-making.

Their romance was brought to an end when the officer's ship was recalled and despatched to another part of the world. The lieutenant was disconsolate and tried many subterfuges in an attempt to get another posting to the eastern Mediterranean. Finally, after more than five years, he did return to Turkey, but found that in his absence Yasmine's infidelity had been betrayed to her husband by the other wives and concubines of the harem and she had paid the penalty which Turkish law prescribed for her offence and had been executed.

When he closed the book, Gautier wondered how much of the story was drawn from Mounet's own experience. He had been in Turkey and had hinted to Gautier that *Seraglio* was the story of the girl whose portrait had a place of honour in his home. On the other hand he was not short of imagination and was probably vain enough to embroider the story so that it enhanced his reputation as a man of the world and a lover. The face of the girl in the portrait was indisputably beautiful but the likeness had been painted at second-hand, and by Boldini, who had a talent for improving on nature, especially when the fee he was being paid was high. Gautier had read *Seraglio* hoping that it might give him an insight into Mounet's character and suggest who, apart from Admiral Pottier, might hate him, but he had learnt nothing.

Pushing the book on one side, he took the pack of cards from his pocket and spread them out on his desk. He had no clear idea of what he proposed to do with the cards and before any plan materialised a messenger from the general office came into the room. Gautier suppressed a smile. Now everyone in the Sûreté would hear that the youngest and most individual of the senior inspectors, whom many considered to be an eccentric, had taken to reading novels and playing cards in his office. The messenger had two messages for him: the first that he was required to be in the director-general's office in ten minutes; the second that there had been another murder which might be connected with the affair of the Fifteen Condemned Ones.

'Who was the victim?' Gautier asked.

'A footman in the service of the Comte and Comtesse de Neuville. He was poisoned.'

In Courtrand's office on the first floor of the building arrangements had been made for a formal conference, with Courtrand, the four senior inspectors and Courtrand's secretary, a self-effacing little man with a waspish tongue named Corbin, all seated around a table which had been brought into the office solely for that purpose.

'You will all have heard the news,' Courtrand said. 'Now there have been five people assassinated and a sixth attempt which failed. The situation is becoming intolerable.' None of the inspectors seemed inclined to contradict this judgement, so he continued, 'I have read your reports and I have to say that the people you were to warn yesterday do not appear to have been unduly alarmed by the threat to their lives. I find myself wondering whether you were forcible enough in impressing on them the gravity of the situation.'

'The two I spoke to,' one of the inspectors said, 'thought the list of Condemned Ones was just a hoax.'

'Don't they understand that to anarchists all people of good standing, all owners of property, are enemies?'

'Do you still believe that this is the work of anarchists, Monsieur le Directeur?'

'Certainly. There can be no doubt about that. Who else but a group of anarchists would wish to kill so

64

many people? They seek to undermine the fabric of our society, to destroy the republic and replace it with – well, of course, with anarchy. Yes, I know you will tell me that there have been no anarchist outrages in France for more than a decade. That's true and it is largely because of the efficiency of this department. But anarchism is not dead. Anarchists have been at work all over Europe and now we can expect their return to France. Why, only this morning my barber told me that he had seen two bearded men in long cloaks hurrying along the street in which he lives.'

For Courtrand to give the Sûreté the credit for stamping out anarchy in France was as absurd as it was typical of the man. Several other factors were responsible, not least public outrage at the assassination of the President of the Republic which had led to the passing of a draconian law against anarchists and other subversives. It was also typical of Courtrand to seize on what his barber had told him as proof that what he, without any evidence, had concluded was the truth. The barber, who went to Courtrand's home twice a week to trim his beard and moustaches, would have heard about the bombs on the houseboat and in the law courts and would have told his client what he thought he would like to hear. Anarchists were universally believed to have unkempt beards and wear long cloaks, under which they were supposed to conceal their explosives.

'Then what action do you propose that we should take, Monsieur?' another of the inspectors asked.

'I have a plan,' Courtrand said, in the manner of Napoleon explaining his tactics to his generals. 'A first principle of criminal investigation is that any crime committed by a group of people is vulnerable to discovery, because it cannot be kept a secret for long. Someone will betray it, either deliberately or by carelessness – an accomplice resentful because he has not had his share of the spoils, a spiteful wife whose husband has been unfaithful, one of the criminals who drinks too much and grows boastful. What we must do is search and probe and pry until we find the weak link, the Judas.'

'But that could take time, weeks even!'

'Not if we act with urgency, using all the resources at our command. This is what we will do.'

Courtrand's plan was that each of the four senior inspectors would be given a different assignment. One would trace all former anarchists known to be still living in France as well as all relatives and associates of those who had been guillotined or imprisoned and interrogate them rigorously. Another inspector would do the same for all socialists and other subversives who had entered France within the last three years. A third would concentrate on the editors and staffs of the radical newspapers and revues and all those who had contributed articles to them. Each inspector would have as many men as he needed to assist him and each would be allocated a substantial budget to be used to mobilise the very considerable number of police informers in the Paris underworld.

As he listened to Courtrand, Gautier began to feel for the first time a measure of respect for the man. What he said about crimes committed by a group of people was certainly true, but Gautier had never supposed that Courtrand, whose appointment as head of the Sûreté had been a piece of political patronage, a return for favours done, would ever have thought seriously about the theory of detection. His plan for dealing with the affair of the fifteen was also sound, assuming that it was a plot contrived by anarchists, but Gautier did not believe that to be the case.

'The last assignment,' Courtrand concluded, 'is one for you, Gautier. You will conduct a routine investigation into all the assassinations that have taken place so far and into any that may occur in the future. Collect all the reports on these cases, including your own, and build up a dossier on each. Study each murder carefully, the method

66

of killing, the place, the time, the people involved either directly or by chance, to see if you can find any common link between them. Send out men to look for witnesses and have them brought in for examination. Three examining magistrates will be appointed and you will work directly under them.'

The assignment he had been given was the one which appealed to Gautier least. Much of the work would need to be done in his office, collecting and sifting facts, and what attracted him to police work was not facts but people. He liked talking to people and even more he liked listening to them, hearing their opinions, their likes and dislikes, their prejudices and their boasting. From what he heard he could analyse their strengths and their weaknesses and form his own assessment of their character and of the motives behind their actions. Although he was disappointed at the assignment he had been given, he was not surprised by it. Courtrand had used the expression 'routine investigation' with a special emphasis. He believed in routine as the basis for all police work as unshakeably as other men believed in the Holy Trinity, and his constant complaint was that Gautier too often ignored the rules of procedure and used his own unorthodox methods. So he had given him the assignment which would allow him the least freedom and which would keep him busy trying to meet the demands of not one but three *juges d'instruction*.

'And now, Messieurs,' Courtrand said, standing up. 'Let us start work with all speed. Remember that time is what we have to fight if we are to save many lives.'

When the other inspectors left the room, Gautier remained behind. 'What is it Gautier?' Courtrand asked impatiently.

'I wondered what you could tell me of this latest murder, Monsieur, at the home of the Comte de Neuville.'

'I only know what the police from the local commissariat have reported: that a footman in the service of the

Comtesse was found dead in his bed this morning. It seems he had been poisoned.'

'Do we know his name?'

'Yes, and it is not on the list of the Fifteen Condemned Ones, though that may not be significant. But don't stay gossiping here, Gautier. Get round to the count's home at once.'

As Gautier turned to go there was a knock on the door and a uniformed policeman came in, looking flustered. 'I apologise for interrupting you, Monsieur le Directeur,' he said.

'You knew I was in conference!'

'Yes, Monsieur, but there is a gentleman outside who insists on seeing you at once. When we asked him to wait he grew very angry.'

'Who is it?' The policeman held out a visiting card and when Courtrand read it he said, 'Then ask the gentleman to come in.'

The visitor was Jacques Mounet. He was conventionally dressed in a morning coat which showed what the Turkish robes and bedouin garb had concealed, that he was a small man but well developed, as though he had devoted a good deal of time to callisthenics. He was similar in build to his cousin Pierre but in looks there was no resemblance whatsoever. Jacques had a sharper, more intelligent face and the watchful eyes of someone who observes life all the time, even when he is living it.

'Monsieur Mounet! An honour!' Courtrand's indignation had been replaced by obsequiousness. 'I am at your disposal. What can I do for you?'

'Have you heard that one of the Comte de Neuville's servants was poisoned last night?'

'Regrettably, yes. We have.'

Taking out a handkerchief Mounet wiped away the sweat which had formed not on his brow but above his upper lip. He had the look of a man who had been badly frightened and his hand shook. 'Then what are you going to do about it?'

'Inspecteur Gautier is leaving even now to start an investigation.'

'You realise of course that the man was poisoned by mistake.'

'By mistake?'

'Of course! The poison was intended for me.'

The Comte and Comtesse de Neuville, or, to give them their true name, Neuville-Ferran, lived in Avenue du Bois, not far from the home of Paul Valanis. Their house, designed by France's leading architect, had been built not many years previously, paid for out of the fortune of the countess, daughter of an American railroad millionaire, and furnished with paintings, furniture and objets d'art from all over Europe chosen by the count. The count was an aesthete and minor poet, thought by many to be more interested in the company of beautiful young men than in that of women, but he had fulfilled his part of the marriage contract by giving his wife not only one of the oldest titles in France, but two children. When Gautier arrived the count received him in his study.

'So the Sûreté has decided at last to take an interest in this disgraceful business,' he said peevishly. 'The local police have done nothing.'

'It is most regrettable.'

'Regrettable? Is that all you can say? Do you realise what this poisoning in my house will mean? People will not feel safe dining here. Already two people who had accepted invitations for next week have sent their excuses.'

'But how could they have heard about it so soon?'

The count snorted contemptuously. 'My dear Gautier, the servants have their own telegraph system, much more rapid and efficient than anything the Americans ever invented.'

'One of your guests at dinner last night, Monsieur Jacques Mounet, believes the poison was intended for him.'

At the Sûreté that morning Mounet had persisted in his claim that he had been the poisoner's intended victim, although his only reason for believing so seemed to be that his name was on the list of Condemned Ones. His answers to the questions which Courtrand and Gautier had asked him had been vague and confused and he had not been able to suggest which of the other dinner guests or which of the count's servants might have wished to kill him.

'The man's a coward! Clever and talented he may be but he's a coward.' Although the count was an aesthete he was also a fine swordsman and he was proud of his ancestors who had fought courageously for successive kings of France. 'It's obvious that the poisoning was an accident.'

'An accident? How could that be?'

'Negligence by one of the tradesmen from whom we buy our supplies. The food could easily have been contaminated with some poisonous substance. You know how careless these people are.'

'Surely in that case others in your house who ate the same food would have been affected.'

'Not necessarily. The servants eat at different times and they do not eat the same food as us. They may not even eat the same food as each other but prepare their own.'

'We shall explore every possibility and no doubt your servants may be able to help us. At the same time we must also take into account Monsieur Mounet's allegations.'

'But who on earth would wish to poison him?'

'He says he has enemies. Do you have a list of your guests who dined with you last night?'

'That's absurd! I do not have poisoners for friends.'

'Even so.'

'I do not have a list but I can tell you who was there. We were twelve in all.'

The count recited the names of the guests who had dined at his home the previous evening. They were all drawn from letters or the arts, authors, musicians and artists. Apart from Mounet only one among them was on the list of Condemned Ones. That was Ivan Grigov, the Russian singer who, the Sûreté had now established, was currently in Paris singing at l'Opéra.

'The best thing you can do,' the count said, crossing the room to a bell-pull on the wall, 'is to talk to my butler. He will be able to tell you the circumstances of my footman's death and exactly what took place in the servants' quarters last night.'

A footman dressed in the blue and silver livery of the count's family appeared and led Gautier to the servants' quarters where the butler had a small room from which he ran the household, supervising the work of the footmen, maids, a cook and kitchen maids, two coachmen who drove the carriages, grooms and a chauffeur for the new automobile. As Gautier passed through the kitchens he could sense in the faces and in the silence of the other servants the mingled fear and fascination which unexpected death always aroused in those close to it.

The butler was an elderly man who had served the count's family for many years. He listened composedly to the questions that Gautier asked and his answers were precise and unemotional. The staff, he said, always had their evening meal before dinner was served to the family and guests. They did not eat the same food as was served in the dining room, but had a meal prepared for them by the cook, and their own wine. The footman who had been poisoned had eaten and drunk the same as all the other servants. As the senior footman, the man had a bedroom on his own and he had been found dead there that morning. No other member of the staff had heard any noises in

71

the night, although it was apparent that the dead man had vomited and his body had been found, contorted by pain, sprawled on the floor.

'Have you no idea of how he might have come to be poisoned?' Gautier asked the butler.

'I have been considering the matter, Monsieur, and I can think of only one possible explanation. Some of the gentlemen who dined with us last night stayed on after the ladies had left and the Comtesse had retired. They and the Comte were up until well after midnight, drinking cognac and talking. The footman who died was on duty and he had to stay up to show the guests out of the house. He also tidied the room after they had gone and took the brandy glasses back to the scullery.'

'Are you suggesting that he drank some of the cognac as well?'

'I cannot say whether he did or not but it is always possible that one of the gentlemen left a half-full glass. It was the very best old cognac.' The butler shrugged expressively.

'What happened to the glasses?'

'Regrettably, Monsieur, they were all washed by one of the kitchen maids early this morning. It was only later that we learnt that the footman had been poisoned.'

'Who had been pouring the cognac for the guests who stayed behind?'

'The Comte would have done, unless he told them to help themselves. I took a decanter of cognac and glasses to them before I retired.'

Gautier told the butler that if the decanter of cognac had not already been emptied and rinsed out, it should be locked away. Later that morning he would arrange for it to be collected and taken for analysis. He did not believe it likely, though, that the analysts would find anything, for if the cognac in the decanter had been poisoned, some of the other guests would have drunk it and been affected as well.

'Do you know which of the guests stayed late?' he asked the butler.

'Yes, Monsieur.'

'Then I would like you to write down their names and also to give me a list of all your staff in this household.'

'I expected that you would want a list of the household and have prepared one.' The butler handed Gautier the list. 'To write down the names of the guests who stayed late will take only a few seconds.'

'Excellent!'

As the butler began writing, Gautier looked at the list of the household staff which he had been given. He did not expect that the names would mean anything to him, but one did catch his eye. 'Who is this F. Dubois?' he asked.

'Madame Françoise Dubois, Monsieur. She is our cook.'

There had been a Dubois on the list of Condemned Ones, Gautier recalled, but that might be no more than coincidence. Dubois was a common name in France and he could not even guess how many hundred people of that name there might be in Paris.

'Tell me about the footman,' he told the butler. 'What kind of man was he?'

André, the footman, had been a thoroughly dependable man according to the butler; a conscientious worker who never shirked his duties and who had always been ready to lend a hand to any of the other servants who might be overworked. He was generous, too, and his only fault, if he had one, was his fondness for the fine wines in his master's cellar. More than once the butler had found cause to admonish him for being too free with a half-empty bottle of Bordeaux that had come back to the kitchen.

'Did he have a wife?'

'No, but he was betrothed. He was to marry a nice young girl who is in service with a wealthy foreign lady, the Princesse Sophia Dashkova.'

73

7

The Cercle St Honoré was a club whose members were drawn mainly from past and present senior officers of the army and navy. Although not as exclusive as the Jockey Club, it was regarded favourably by Paris society and membership of it would help to give an entrée to drawing rooms where professional soldiers and sailors might not otherwise be accepted. The club, which was not in rue St Honoré but in rue de Rivoli, was run on the lines of a gentleman's club in London, and as he went up the steps to the entrance, Gautier wondered why the French, most of whom either distrusted or hated the English, could not resist imitating their manners, their dress and their institutions.

When he had arrived back at the Sûreté after visiting the home of the Comte de Neuville, he had found waiting for him a *'petit bleu'*, or message sent through the pneumatic telegraph system of Paris. The message was from Admiral Pottier and it asked whether Inspector Gautier would be kind enough to meet him at the Cercle St Honoré as soon as possible. Recalling the admiral's mention at Madame Mauberge's salon of a problem that was troubling him and his denial of their conversation when they had met at Princesse Sophia's apartment the following evening, Gautier wondered whether the old man's memory was no longer reliable or whether, as well as being a womaniser, he was one of the many eccentrics in Paris society.

He found the admiral waiting for him with a glass of cognac and a cigar in the smoking room of the club which overlooked the Jardin des Tuileries. Gautier had heard

74

that in London clubmen habitually dozed at their clubs during the afternoons, but apart from Admiral Pottier the smoking room of the Cercle St Honoré was empty and he suspected that Frenchmen, if they wished to sleep off the effects of too good a lunch, would prefer to do so in the bed of a *petite amie* whom they had installed in a convenient apartment nearby. The admiral pointed towards a chair opposite to his own but did not offer Gautier either a brandy or a cigar.

'As I mentioned to you, Gautier, I have a troublesome little problem which I wish to resolve.'

'But Admiral, yesterday you said you had no such problem!'

'My dear fellow, that was in front of Princesse Sophia. She is a foreigner of course and we Frenchmen should keep our troubles to ourselves.'

'What is the nature of your problem, Monsieur?'

'It concerns a lady and for that reason must be handled with discretion.'

'That goes without saying.'

'The lady is being pestered by the unwelcome attentions of a man – I will not call him a gentleman – and I have decided she should be freed of them.'

'So you want the police to intervene?'

'Not exactly.'

'Then how can I be of service to you?'

Admiral Pottier looked down into his glass thoughtfully as he swirled the brandy gently around it. One sensed that he had a proposition to make or a favour to ask which had to be carefully phrased, and that skill with words was not his forte. He was a large man with a broad, insensitive face and large, capable hands, who gave the impression of impatiently wanting to be active.

'In your position, Inspecteur, one supposes that you must come into contact with unscrupulous characters.'

'Too many, unfortunately.'

75

'And some among them no doubt are physically formidable and not averse to violence.'

'There are some who appear to enjoy it.'

'I am looking for two, perhaps three such men. They would be given an assignment for which they would be handsomely paid.'

Gautier stared at Pottier incredulously. 'You are not planning to have this man assaulted? The one who is pestering the lady?'

'Why not? He does not have to be killed or even maimed, but a good beating would teach him a lesson. I would prefer to settle matters in another way, but the pig ignored my challenge to a duel.'

'Monsieur,' Gautier said sharply, 'I am a police officer. You cannot expect me to become involved in an affair of this nature.'

'I cannot see why not. Are not the police supposed to provide citizens with protection?'

'But you are asking me to take part in a criminal act!'

'There is no reason why you should be involved. Just give me the names of suitable men and I will make all the arrangements.'

'Condoning a crime is as bad as committing one.'

'Then you refuse?'

'I do, Monsieur. Absolutely!'

'You are making a mistake, Inspecteur. I still have influential friends who would be useful to you – in the matter of promotion for example.'

'Even so.'

'You will regret your intransigence!'

As he went down the stairs out of the club, Gautier was smiling. The admiral's threat did not worry him unduly, for he had offended important people before. Indeed Courtrand often accused him of doing so deliberately, out of perversity. In Gautier's experience people who boasted of their influence almost always turned out to have less than they believed. What amused and mildly astonished him was not that Pottier wished to have a philanderer taught a painful lesson, but his naïvety in supposing that the police would be a party to it. For what he had in mind the admiral would do better to look to the navy for assistance, for there was no shortage of thugs in the lower deck and plenty of officers eager for promotion to act as a go-between.

When he arrived at the Sûreté he was told by the policeman on duty at the entrance that a lady had been asking for him. The lady had refused to go in and wait in Gautier's office, but was waiting instead in her carriage. The man pointed to a smart little coupé, drawn by two horses and with a top-hatted coachman on the driving seat on the opposite side of quai des Orfèvres. Gautier thought he recognised the coupé and was not surprised when he reached it to find Michelle Le Tellier inside. She was wearing a veil, a precaution against being recognised by her friends when she was compromising herself by waiting for a man. As soon as Gautier climbed in beside her, the coupé moved on, the coachman obeying the instructions she must have given him beforehand.

'Now I have to come and find you,' she said reproachfully.

'I did not know you wished to see me.'

'There was a time when you did not wait to be told,' she replied, untruthfully, for he had never once gone to her home uninvited. 'You who were so attentive now wait on others.'

'What others?'

'They say you were dining with Princesse Sophia last night.'

'I went to see the princess at her request.'

'What did she want?'

'I think she was only using me to get rid of an unwelcome admirer.'

Michelle seemed satisfied with the answer, which led Gautier to believe that the princess's stratagem must be one commonly employed by other ladies. She said, 'I came to see you because I wanted to be sure that I could count on you for Monday.'

'What's happening on Monday?'

'The Duchesse de Chalon's masked ball. Jean-Paul, don't tell me you have forgotten!'

'I had forgotten, but of course I will be enchanted to escort you to the ball.'

'But it's the Duchesse de Chalon! And she sent you an invitation!'

There was a subtle nuance in Michelle's reproach which Gautier found ironic. In the short time since she had come out of mourning, he had been with Michelle to more than one social event, but in every case it had been she who had invited him to escort her. For the duchess's masked ball he had been sent a personal invitation, which must be an accolade he supposed, but even so the invitation had not been sent to him personally but to Michelle Le Tellier to pass on to him, and that was probably one reason why he had forgotten about the ball. He did not blame the Duchesse de Chalon or her secretary, for he had made no attempt to get the address of his apartment into the address books of fashionable hostesses, not because he was ashamed of the *quartier* in which he lived, but because he had never seen any permanent place for himself in society. For Michelle, however, the fact that the invitation had been sent through her proved that he had only been invited on her account. He should be grateful and certainly not forget either the invitation or his obligation to her.

'You would be advised, *chéri*,' she said, 'not to become too friendly with Princesse Sophia.'

'I would say that's very unlikely.'

'Those who welcomed her into Paris society are becoming a little disenchanted.'

'Why should that be?'

'She failed to carry out her commitments and some people have suffered as a result.'

'In what way?'

The princess, Michelle told Gautier, had aspirations to being a patron of the arts and she had planned to bring an opera company which she had formed in St Petersburg to Paris that season. Arrangements had been made for the company to appear in a Paris theatre, performing new Russian operas, as well as some of the great classics of Verdi, Mozart and Rossini – not Wagner, for the chauvinistic French were still hostile to the great German composer. At the last minute, Michelle said, the arrangements for the visit had fallen through, the princess had reneged on her obligations and those who had been backing her in France had all lost money.

'Did she give no reason for failing to bring the opera company?' Gautier asked.

'Not a very convincing one. She claims that one of the singers, on whom the whole success of the tour depended, refused to honour his contract. The bass, Ivan Grigov.'

That afternoon there was a development in the matter of the bomb that had exploded in the Palais de Justice. It was one of those unexpected strokes of good fortune on which the police often had to rely in solving difficult cases. A clerk who worked in the law courts reported having seen a man carrying a package in a corridor which led to Judge Lacaze's court not long before the bomb exploded. The good fortune was that the clerk had a good memory and he recognised the man with the package as one he had seen in the Palais de Justice almost fifteen years previously. Edouard Ribot was a watchmaker who had given evidence at the trial of two anarchists charged with planting a series of bombs in different parts of Paris. One of the accused, he had told the court, had paid him to make a supply of simple clockwork devices which, after being wound up, would activate a trigger after an interval of about five minutes. He claimed that he had been told the devices were required for scientific experiments in a laboratory and had been satisfied that this was true. The authorities had not seriously believed that part of his story and in different circumstances Ribot himself might have been on trial as an accomplice in the bombings, but his evidence had been needed to secure the conviction of the anarchists and their subsequent execution by guillotine.

Since then Ribot appeared to have behaved himself, but the police had kept a check on him and as soon as the clerk in the law courts had reported seeing him, he was brought in and questioned by a *juge d'instruction*. Gautier had been present at the interrogation and was afterwards given a copy of the official account of the proceedings. Now, in his office, he began reading it.

MINISTRY OF JUSTICE

Dossier No: 0003

Explosion of bomb in the Palais de Justice

Question: A witness has identified you, Ribot, as a man whom he saw in a corridor in the Palais de Justice shortly after midday yesterday. Do you admit to being there at that time?

Ribot: I do.

Question: And for what purpose were you there?

Ribot: I was on my way to the public gallery of a court in which a case of fraud was being tried.

Question: And of what interest was that case to you?

Ribot: Criminal law has always had a special

80

interest for me. I often wish that I had entered the legal profession.

Question: You are a watchmaker. How could you have aspired to being a lawyer?

Ribot: My father had the opportunity to place me as a clerk to a lawyer. He believed watchmaking would be a more honourable occupation.

Question: Mocking the legal profession will not help you in your present circumstances. Are you saying that you went to the Palais de Justice merely to watch this trial for fraud?

Ribot: Yes. There was a similar case some years ago that is mentioned in the legal textbooks. I wished to see if the outcome in this case would be the same.

Question: Few people will believe you, but we will leave that for the time being. It is reported that when you were seen in the corridor you were carrying a package. What was it?

Ribot: I have no idea.

Question: How can that be?

Ribot: It was like this. On my way to the court I was stopped by a stranger outside the Palais de Justice. He asked me where I was going and when I told him he gave me the package. I was to give it to a man who would be waiting by the entrance of Judge Lacaze's court. The man explained that he was in a hurry and did not have time to take the package there himself.

Question: And you agreed?

Ribot: Why not? I have always found that it pays to be helpful.

Question: How were you to recognise the man to

	whom you were to give the package?
Ribot:	I was told he would have a black beard.
Question:	And be wearing a broad-brimmed hat and an anarchist's cloak, I suppose?
Ribot:	No, but he would have a carnation in his buttonhole.
Question:	And did you find this man there?
Ribot:	No. When I reached the court there was no one of that description to be seen. Soon afterwards Judge Lacaze adjourned the trial for a lunch break, so I left the package where I thought the man was certain to find it.
Question:	Do you seriously expect us to believe this unlikely story?
Ribot:	Why not? What else could I do? I was not prepared to take the package with me.
Question:	Do you realise that the package must have contained a bomb?
Ribot:	In view of what happened afterwards it seems likely that it did, but how was I to know that?
Question:	Your story is impossible to believe, but let us assume it is true. Describe the man who gave you the package.

The description which Ribot had given of the man he claimed had given him the bomb was so vague that it was valueless. The account of the *juge d'instruction*'s examination continued for several pages, but Gautier did not bother to read it. Many of the questions which Ribot had been asked were merely variations on those he had been asked before, rephrased in the hope that they might trap him into contradictions and so prove he had been lying, but the watchmaker was not to be trapped. Gautier was about to add the transcript to the small pile of papers he had already accumulated in the dossier of the case, which would now start to grow rapidly to satisfy the regulations of French legal bureaucracy, when Surat came into the office and he passed it to him instead.

When Surat had read the first few pages he commented, 'Ribot's story is ridiculous, but it will be difficult to disprove.'

'Yes. Like all the best lies it probably has some truth. No doubt he was asked to take the package into the Palais de Justice, or at least he was paid to take it.'

'But he must have known it was a bomb.'

'Of course. He will have made the bomb himself. One thing puzzles me though.'

'What's that?'

'Why did he plant the bomb in the court at that time of day? He must have known that the trial would be adjourned at lunch time.'

'He may have thought that there would be less chance of his being seen carrying it in at that time.'

'I suppose so,' Gautier agreed, but Surat could see that he was not convinced by the explanation.

'This Ribot has been detained and will be questioned again I suppose.'

'No. The *juge d'instruction* agreed with me that we should leave him at liberty for the time being but keep him under surveillance. That way he might lead us to whomever it was who paid him to make the bomb.'

Privately Gautier thought that there was only the slenderest chance of Ribot betraying the person or people behind the bombing of the Palais de Justice, for the watchmaker had shown he was cool and resourceful. Moreover, it was unlikely that he even knew who had paid for the bomb to be made and planted in Judge Lacaze's court. There would have been a go-between. Napoleon was supposed to have said that the English were a nation of shopkeepers, but in Gautier's experience no nation was more commercially minded than the French. In Paris it was possible to get almost any little commission carried out expeditiously. The concierge at a hotel would know where to get a traveller's valise repaired; if one of a team of horses pulling a carriage threw a shoe in the centre of the city, a passing policeman could recommend an honest blacksmith; if the string of a lady's pearls broke in a restaurant there would be a waiter who could have them restrung while dinner was being served. Anything and everything could be arranged, quietly, quickly and for only a modest commission to the go-between. And what was true for commerce was also true for crime. One could always find a go-between to put one in touch with a man with a knife, an expert in arson or a watchmaker who made bombs.

'What are your instructions for me then, patron?' Surat asked.

'We will leave bombs for the present and turn our attention to the arts.'

'The arts?'

'To the opera to be more precise. A Russian singer named Ivan Grigov is at present performing in Paris. Make enquiries discreetly and find out what you can about him.'

'Is that all?'

'No. I have two other tasks for you. You need not do them yourself, and use as many men as you need to assist you.'

The first task, he told Surat, was to have enquiries made at every place along the Seine in Paris where boats were moored. The man whom he had seen appearing from behind Valanis's houseboat just before the bomb exploded had been in a rowing boat, which meant that he could not have come from very far. Either he owned a boat which he kept on the Seine or he had hired or stolen one. In any event it should be possible to trace it.

'The second task is rather more urgent,' Gautier told

Surat, 'and here again I would prefer it if the gentleman concerned did not know we were making enquiries about his movements, at least for the present. Try to find out where Astrux, the fortune teller, was in the early hours of the morning when that bomb exploded on the houseboat. He may have spent the night away from home or he may have risen early and gone out. The servants in his household may know.'

'Does that mean he is suspected of having planted that bomb?'

Gautier shrugged his shoulders. 'He seems to have had a motive for doing so.'

8

Next morning, on his way to the Sûreté, before crossing Pont Neuf, Gautier walked along the embankment to look at Valanis's houseboat. Workmen were busy repairing the damage and they may well have been working through the night as a number of lamps had been set up on the deck and others fixed to the superstructure. Most of the damaged part of the hull and deck had been cut away and new bulkheads and partitioning were being fitted in the area below deck. As he was watching, Gautier heard his name being called.

'Inspecteur, would you care to join me for breakfast?'

Pierre Mounet was standing on deck towards the bows of the boat and he waved. Gautier had not recognised him because he was wearing overalls and the grease on his hands suggested that he had been doing his share of the work that was being done to repair the boat. When Gautier went on board they went below and Mounet led him along a passageway to the dining saloon.

'You go in,' he said, 'and I'll join you when I've washed.'

Gautier remembered the dining saloon from his previous visit to the houseboat. Like the rest of the passenger accommodation it was sumptuously furnished with furniture, carpets and curtains that would not have been out of place in the finest homes in Paris. The décor had changed, though, and one suspected that Valanis had it changed as often as he changed his mistresses, trying perhaps to suit their tastes or even to match their colouring. On one wall there was a blank space where, Gautier recalled, had hung a

86

particularly striking portrait of the Princesse de Caramond, which had been commissioned by Valanis from a leading portrait painter. Presently Mounet came in carrying a tray with a pot of coffee, fresh bread, butter and conserves. They sat down to eat and Gautier was amused when he saw that the table in the saloon was bolted to the floor as it might be in an ocean liner, although it was inconceivable that the houseboat would ever take to sea at any distance from the shore or in any waves worthy of the name.

'A traditional French breakfast is the finest breakfast in the world,' Mounet said, as he poured the coffee. 'Do you know that the English ruin their digestions by eating ham and eggs and porridge in the mornings?'

'So I believe. It's barbaric!'

'As you can see I have decided to stay on in Paris so I can supervise the repairs to the boat.'

'Where are you staying? With your cousin?'

'No, in the small hotel on the Left Bank where I always stay when I visit Paris on business. I could not impose on Jacques,' Mounet replied. He paused and glanced at Gautier as though he wondered whether his explanation was enough. Then he added, 'In any case Jacques and I have never been very close.'

'He was away in the navy for several years I suppose.'

'That isn't the only reason. There was a split in our family several years ago over the business.'

'The shipbuilding business?'

'Yes, though as I told you we build boats, not ships.'

Mounet's father, he told Gautier, and the father of his cousin Jacques were brothers who had inherited a business in Le Havre building small vessels, fishing boats and tugs and coastal patrol vessels for the navy and the coast-guards. The company had been reasonably successful, but it became less so when some of the larger shipbuilding firms moved into what had always been a profitable sector of marine business. Building small ships did not require such a large investment of capital and brought a quicker turn-over.

'When the firm's orders began to fall off,' Mounet said, 'and the income from it started to diminish, my uncle, Jacques's father, decided he wished to pull out.'

'To sell his part of the company?'

'Yes. He thought he would be able to use the money more profitably in other business ventures. My uncle was something of a gambler, you must understand. Unfortunately, although not surprisingly, he could not find anyone willing to buy his share of the firm.'

'So what happened?'

'Eventually my father bought him out. My father did not wish to and could not really afford to, but my uncle persuaded him. He had difficulty in raising the money, had to mortgage everything he owned and borrow from the banks. It took him years to pay off the debts he incurred.'

'And how did your uncle fare?'

'Successfully at first. He made one or two spectacular coups with investments. Then he lost a great deal of money in the Panama Canal collapse.'

Gautier had been too young at the time to remember much about the financial disaster which occurred when the company building the Panama Canal went into liquidation in 1889. He knew, however, that hundreds of small investors lost their money and the collapse of the company was followed by a major political scandal when members of the Government were accused of being fraudulently involved.

'Worse followed,' Mounet continued. 'In a despairing effort to save himself from bankruptcy, my uncle persuaded local people in Le Havre to put money into a venture which, to say the least of it, was dubious if not an actual swindle. When it failed and he was threatened with prosecution, he shot himself.'

'How dreadful for your cousin!'

For a time neither man spoke. Mounet may have been recalling the horror of his uncle's suicide and the devastating impact it must have had on a close-knit family. Gautier was wondering why Mounet had told him the story. For what reason had he felt it necessary to explain why he and his cousin were not on the best of terms?

'Jacques and I were at the same school at the time,' Mounet went on, 'and though my own family were struggling to pay their way, I was not asked to make the same sacrifices that Jacques did. The clothes he wore were second-hand, bought after other boys had outgrown them and often mended time after time, and he never had any money to spend on boyish treats. I believe he resented it.'

'It was not your fault nor that of your family.'

'I know, but he may not have been told the full story. He was very young at the time.'

'And he has not forgotten his resentment after all these years?'

'I'm sure he has, but rifts are difficult to heal, particularly in families. Pride gets in the way.'

Gautier knew that Mounet was right. He himself had two aunts, once devoted sisters, who had quarrelled over some trivial issue more than thirty years ago. Now, both widows, they lived facing each other in a small village, but never spoke to each other, nor even nodded when they passed in the street. All the combined efforts of the family to effect a reconciliation, make them see sense and give each other companionship in their old age, had been in vain.

'I have always admired my cousin,' Mounet said. 'By sheer willpower and determination he got himself accepted by the navy and he worked enormously hard to build up his physique, so that he could hold his own in a career for which he was never really suited. And he was devoted to his mother. He kept the family home going by personal sacrifices and supported not only his mother but her two sisters.'

89

'His mother is no longer alive then?'

'No, the sad part of it is that she did not live long enough to enjoy his success. She died not long ago. Jacques was devastated, inconsolable.'

'Was she living with him in Paris at the time?'

'No. My aunt hated Paris. Jacques had their family home enlarged and refurbished, but soon afterwards she died,' Mounet replied, and then he added, 'In a strange way, her death seems to have blunted Jacques's resentment and softened his bitterness. I believe now that we can be friends again. When he heard that I was in Paris he sent me a charming note, offering to see that I am received in society while I am here. He says he can arrange for me to be invited to dinner parties, soirées and other social events.'

'How kind of him. When was that?'

'The day before yesterday. As a matter of fact the note came round here by hand only a few minutes after you left Monsieur Valanis and me.'

'But will you have time for social events?'

'Oh yes. As you can see I have been working alongside the men but as soon as the structural repairs are finished I will be able to leave them in the evenings at least.'

'Even though the vessel has to be ready in a week?'

Mounet laughed. 'That's impossible! A fantasy! The boat should have been towed to Le Havre and put into dry dock. As it is we will be able to patch her up, but it will take at least two weeks, more probably three.'

Gautier saw no point in remarking that the owner of the vessel would not be pleased to hear what Mounet was saying. He knew from his past encounters with him that Valanis did not like to be thwarted and if, as one might assume, his latest mistress was to be a guest on the impending cruise, he would be impatient to start. When they had finished breakfast, Mounet took Gautier round the houseboat and showed him the work that had to be done. In addition to the structural damage which the explosion had caused in the stern of the vessel, the effects of the fire it had started could be seen amidships. The panelling in the main saloon was badly warped and would have to be replaced, while the carpets and curtains had been first singed by the heat and then damaged by water from the hoses of the fire brigade. Only the owner's stateroom and the cabins towards the bows of the houseboat were totally unaffected.

'One invitation I hope my brother can arrange for me is to the races at Longchamp tomorrow,' Mounet said when Gautier was about to leave.

'Why? Are you a betting man?'

'Heavens no! Not after seeing how gambling can ruin a life. It is simply that I have never been horse-racing and I wish to know at least a little about it. Enough to hold an intelligent conversation, no more.'

'You have racing friends?'

'No, but I shall be with racing people shortly. Some time ago I decided in my business to specialise in building pleasure craft and we have been very successful. We have built yachts and cruisers for many wealthy customers, including one for the King of England. Edward was so pleased with the boat we designed and built for him that he has invited my wife and me to go to the regatta at Cowes in England. We will be living as his guests and, as you know, Edward and his friends are very fond of horse-racing.'

'Congratulations! It is a great honour you have been paid.'

When they were shaking hands at the gangplank of the boat Gautier remarked, 'I see the name of the houseboat has been changed.'

'Yes. As you may have guessed Antoinette is the name of a young lady who is a special friend of Monsieur Valanis.'

'I daresay it won't be the last time that the vessel is rechristened.'

'I'm sure you're right,' Mounet replied, grinning.

Gautier did not go directly to the Sûreté, but found a *fiacre* whose driver, sleepy and grumpy after working for the better part of the night, agreed only reluctantly to take him to the offices of *Figaro*. The previous day he had sent Duthrey a message asking if he could arrange for a member of the newspaper's staff to sift through back numbers and collect all the reports it had published on Astrux's trial for libel and also any other news items or articles about the fortune-teller which had appeared within the last two years.

When he reached the offices he found that Duthrey was not there but the articles and clippings for which he had asked were laid out ready for him. He was astonished at the size of the pile. *Figaro* had reported the trial very fully, and as he read the accounts Gautier could not help feeling that the judge and the press had been severe on Astrux, reading more into his predictions about the President than he had said or implied. If Astrux were still aggrieved over the result of the trial one could sympathise with him.

The other stories which *Figaro* had printed about Astrux during the last two years were a striking proof of the extraordinary success that he had achieved in his chosen *métier*. A very large number of people from the upper echelons of Paris society – duchesses, actresses, artists, politicians, impresarios – had consulted him, and a surprisingly high proportion of them had been willing to tell the world how accurate his predictions of the future and how helpful his advice had been to them. Some of the stories, though, were less flattering. Astrux had been unwise enough to tell the Comtesse de Neuville that she would be divorcing her husband for adultery within a year. The countess, after discovering one of her husband's infidelities, had, in a fit of pique, told him what Astrux had predicted, and the count had immediately challenged Astrux to a duel. They had fought with épées early one morning behind the grandstand of the racecourse at Auteuil and Astrux had disgraced himself by seizing his opponent's sword with one hand and using his own to lash out at him as though with a whip. On another occasion the actress Sarah Bernhardt, furious because on his advice she had bought an expensive apartment for a handsome young actor only to find that he was homosexual, arrived in Astrux's apartment early one morning with a horsewhip. He had escaped from her only by jumping out of his bedroom window in his nightshirt. Fortunately the bedroom had been on the first floor of the building, but even so he had broken an ankle in the fall.

What interested Gautier more than the gossip and the scandal was an article which he found among the clippings. Published only two weeks previously under the title 'WHERE DOES OUR FUTURE LIE' and written by Jacques Mounet, it dealt with man's never-ending compulsion to explore his future. Tracing the history of this compulsion, Mounet wrote of the Old Testament prophets and soothsayers, of the astrologers of ancient China, of medieval savants and scholars and of more recent experiments in the occult and the supernatural. The article was cleverly written, in a prose simple enough for anyone to understand, but interspersed with enough quotations to flatter the reader and give an impression of scholarship.

In the final paragraphs Mounet attacked the current vogue for fortune-telling and clairvoyance, pouring scorn on those who professed to be able to read the future and on those gullible enough to believe them. And the sharpest of his ridicule was directed at the man whom he described as 'The Prince of Charlatans'.

'Who is this creature who calls himself The Great Astrux and is insolent enough to compare himself with the great astrologers of the past? He has an imposing figure, certainly, a fine beard and a booming, resonant voice, but behind this façade you will find only the heart of a mouse and the brains of a serving-wench. And what of the art and science which, he claims, allow him to see into the future? His art is on a level with that of the Pétomane, his science no more than that of a gypsy who reads tea-leaves in a travelling fair.'

On his way to the Sûreté, Gautier recalled Mounet telling him that any honest writer made enemies. What he had written would certainly have made an enemy of Astrux. The last sentence of the article contained a particularly offensive insult. The Pétomane was the name adopted by a music-hall performer with an unusual but very successful act. He was able to expel air from his anus at will and, by varying the pitch of the sounds he produced, to play rudimentary tunes, a feat which brought hysterical laughter and cheers from his audiences. Gautier wondered what Astrux had done to provoke Mounet into such a gratuitous attack on his reputation.

When he reached the Sûreté, he found Surat waiting for him. One of the three tasks which Gautier had given him the previous afternoon had been completed. He had learnt from the servants of Astrux that their master had spent the night before the bomb exploded on the houseboat at home.

'Astrux gave a dinner party that evening,' Surat reported, 'and the guests stayed late. And his valet says he was in his bed the following morning. He remembers it because his master had asked to be woken earlier than usual.'

'I wonder why,' Gautier remarked. He was thinking that Astrux could probably have slipped out of his apartment unnoticed and made his way to the Seine, but he could scarcely have slipped back in again without being seen. By the time he would have been returning his servants would have been getting up to start their day's work.

'His valet is sure that Astrux did not use his automobile that night. The chauffeur took it back to its garage quite early.'

'The valet seems to be a talkative fellow.'

'He was, after a few *bocks* in the café yesterday evening.'

'I didn't intend you to be working in the evening again. You should be at home with your family,' Gautier said. The memory of the failure of his own marriage still aroused feelings of guilt. In his obsession with work he had left Suzanne alone too often and had paid for his neglect.

'The evenings are the best time to talk to a valet. Once he has put out his master's evening clothes he is free to go to the café. That's why so many valets get into trouble with drink.'

Gautier had never had and was never likely to have a valet, but he was prepared to believe that what Surat said was true. He listened while Surat went on to report on the other enquiries he had initiated. Four policemen had been sent out that morning to try to trace the rowing boat which Gautier had seen leaving Valanis's houseboat just before the bomb exploded. They would work their way along the river, two covering the right bank and two the left. It would take time, but Surat was sure they would learn the answer. One could not easily hide a rowing boat.

'We've had no success so far with the Russian,' he concluded. 'There is nothing on him in police files.'

'I did not suppose there would be. As far as we know, Grigov is a respectable, law-abiding man, even though he is a Russian.'

Surat appeared disappointed. Like most Frenchmen he was thoroughly suspicious of Russians, associating them at best with wild, drunken debauchery and at worst with bombs and anarchy. When one thought of Russians one did not immediately think of culture.

'Grigov is appearing at l'Opéra,' Gautier told him. 'The people behind the scenes there, stagehands, dressers, ushers, may know something about him. I'm interested in his private life, what he does when he is not singing, what kind of friends he has.'

When Surat left, Gautier realised it was time for him to go to the director-general's office. Courtrand had decided that he would hold a conference every morning at which the senior inspectors would report on the progress they were making in the affair of the Fifteen Condemned Ones. That morning, as the conference began, he was in an equable mood.

'At least, gentlemen, we have had no more bombings or stabbings or poisonings. Perhaps we have frightened these scoundrels off. Tell me, how much closer are we to catching them?'

His mood changed as he listened to each of the inspectors reporting. All the enquiries they had made into known or suspected anarchists had produced nothing. Some were dead, some had left France, a few were in prison, having turned from political crimes to others more likely to bring them material gain. A good many were living peaceably, their fanaticism blunted or gradually engulfed by the mundane preoccupation of earning a livelihood and bringing up a family. There were more enquiries still to be made, more questions to be asked, but so far not one person had been found at whom suspicion might be pointed.

'This is absurd!' Courtrand exclaimed. 'You must have overlooked someone, more than one person no doubt.'

'I cannot help feeling, Monsieur,' Gautier said, 'that this plot is not the work of anarchists.'

'Not again, Gautier!' Courtrand sighed wearily in the manner of a schoolmaster faced with a tiresomely stupid pupil. 'In spite of his denials we know that the bomb in the Palais de Justice must have been made by Ribot. No doubt he made the one that was planted on the houseboat as well. And he has worked for anarchists before.'

'If anarchists were behind it, surely we would have heard more from them. The crimes against society for which the fifteen condemned ones are to be assassinated have never been named. Anarchists like the world to know of their achievements. They thrive on notoriety.'

'Who else but a group of anarchists would have so many intended victims?' one of the other inspectors said. 'Who else would have a motive for wishing to kill fifteen people? Fifteen people from different walks of life who seem to have nothing in common.'

'That's right. Give us a motive, Gautier.'

'Revenge could be the motive. I know of one person who might wish to revenge himself on at least three people on that list.'

'Who? Give us a name.'

'The Great Astrux.'

Gautier had not meant to mention Astrux's name and he was annoyed with himself for allowing the others to manoeuvre him into doing so. Now he had to tell them of the trouble Astrux had caused when he tried to force his way on to Valanis's houseboat and of the article which *Figaro* had published by Jacques Mounet. To his surprise Courtrand did not immediately dismiss the idea that Astrux might be implicated in the plot.

'The man is a scoundrel without doubt,' he commented, 'and his fees are extortionate. Against my advice my wife went to consult him, and for what she was prepared to pay all he would do was to read her future in the cards.' Courtrand suddenly realised what he had said and his face exploded with astonishment. He even smiled. 'Playing cards! That's it! Don't you see? There was a drawing of a playing card against every name on the list of Condemned Ones. Who else would have thought of that? The cards must have some symbolic meaning for him. Gautier, for once you are right! Astrux is responsible for this whole plot. We'll have him brought before a *juge d'instruction* this afternoon and force the truth out of him.'

'Don't you think that would be a little premature, Monsieur?'

'Premature? Why?'

Gautier explained that Astrux had evidently been at home and in bed on the night when the bomb was planted on the houseboat. He also pointed out that there was no evidence whatsoever to link the fortune-teller with the bomb in the Palais de Justice, or the poisoning of the Comte de Neuville's footman, or the stabbings in Pigalle.

'What if we are wrong and Astrux is totally innocent?' he concluded. 'Can you imagine what he would say to the newspapers? We would be made to appear ridiculous.'

Gautier's argument was directed at Courtrand's most vulnerable point. The director-general was inordinately vain and proud. More than anything he dreaded being laughed at.

'We will hold our hand for the time being,' he decided after reflecting for a moment, 'while all of you go out and get the evidence against him that we need. In the mean time Astrux must be kept under surveillance. When he makes his next attack, we shall be ready for him.'

9

Gautier was the first of his group of friends to arrive at the Café Corneille that day. This was unusual, but after he had carried out his share of the instructions Courtrand had given at his morning conference, he could think of nothing he could usefully do. The other inspectors at the meeting had agreed with Courtrand that the first priority must be to find evidence to show that Astrux was implicated in at least the bombing of the houseboat. There were two possibilities; either he had planted the bomb himself or – as in the case of the explosion in the Palais de Justice – paid someone else to do it. If the first were the case, he must have managed to slip out of his house at night, gone down to the Seine and stolen a boat to take the bomb to the houseboat. He would not have had time to go to the houseboat and return before daybreak on foot, and since he had not used his automobile he must have found a *fiacre* to take him. Courtrand had told Gautier to send out enough policemen to question all the drivers of *fiacres* operating in the district where Astrux lived and in the surrounding *quartiers*. This was not such a formidable task as it might appear, since drivers of *fiacres* did in the main operate in one district which could be recognised by the colours of the lamps on their *fiacres*.

To investigate the second possibility, it was decided that Ribot would be recalled before the *juge d'instruction* and confronted with the accusation that he had made and placed both bombs for Astrux. Courtrand had decided that he would be present himself at the examination so that he could help the magistrate in formulating sufficiently intimidating questions, and Gautier was excused from attending. In order to obtain corroborative evidence of the link between Astrux and Ribot, more policemen had been sent to make enquiries around Ribot's place of work, in the hope that someone might be found who had seen Astrux in the vicinity.

Gautier was far from convinced that any of these measures would bear fruit. The frenzy of activity which the fear of more murders and assassinations had triggered off in the Sûreté seemed to him ill-planned and in many respects illogical. The plot behind the murders that had been committed and those that were meant to take place had been carefully constructed and carefully thought out, and reasoned deduction would be needed to unravel and then frustrate it.

While he waited for the other habitués of the Café Corneille to arrive, he took out the pack of playing cards which he now carried with him. The fifteen cards illustrated in the list of Condemned Ones were on top of the pack, for he had spread them out and studied them more than once before. He liked to think that the person or cabal of conspirators behind the plot had dealt a hand of fifteen cards, and he held them in a fan as a card-player would. Five people were now dead, if one included the Comte de Neuville's footman, and if failed attempted murders were counted, one could add Judge Lacaze. He played the cards which had been drawn against the names of these six people, placing them face upwards on the table in front of him. For the count's footman, he used the card which had been drawn against the name F. Dubois. Two other people on the list, Mounet and Grigov, had been at the count's home on the night of the clumsy poisoning attempt, but one had to make assumptions when trying to solve murders and Gautier was prepared to assume that the poison had been intended for Madame

Dubois, the count's cook. The six cards in front of him were:

Apart from the fact that three of the six cards were from the heart suit, he could see nothing in any way out of the ordinary in their arrangement. Six cards could be said to have been played, for although Judge Lacaze had not been killed by the bomb, it did not seem likely that another attempt would be made to kill him since, on the advice of the Prefect of Police, he had gone into hiding. So nine cards remained to be played, nine people to be assassinated. Gautier wondered in what order they would be attacked. With the exception of Judge Lacaze, the targets so far had been ordinary people, of no great importance, one might think. The nine names remaining on the list included the President, a minister, a deputy, a rich businessman and an author, five people of standing, so the next six attacks must include at least two of them.

The thought triggered off another question in his mind. There had been a pause after the first attacks and no new ones had been reported for thirty-six hours. Did that mean they were being executed in batches of six? He discarded the idea, for two batches of six would leave only three names on the list of fifteen. Three batches of five would have been more logical. Picking up the six cards, he added them to the remaining nine and then began placing them face down on the table. He laid a row of five first and then above it a row of four and above that a row of three, then two and finally one, constructing a perfect triangle.

As he laid the last card down, Froissart arrived at the

café and came up to join him. When he saw playing cards in front of Gautier, he smiled.

'French cafés are noted as places for wit and intelligent conversation. One should never be reduced to playing solitaire.'

'I am not playing solitaire, but trying to solve a problem,' Gautier replied, picking up the cards and putting them in his pocket. 'It is the numbers on the cards that interest me.'

'A mathematical problem?'

'One might describe it that way, yes.'

'Then I know the man you should consult. He is perhaps the greatest mathematician of our time. Professor Racine is his name. I often tell him it should be "Racine Carrée", for he can calculate the square-root of any number, however long, in a second.'

While the waiter was fetching his order of a brandy, Froissart explained that Professor Racine was one of those prodigies who were able to do complex mathematical calculations involving numbers with many digits almost instantaneously, but while others with a similar facility had taken their talent to the stage and earned large sums in theatres and music halls, Racine had taken his to the university and to pure mathematics. The professor had been trying to persuade Froissart to publish a book he had written. Froissart had declined, partly because he published mainly poetry and essays of high literary quality, but also because the theme of Racine's thesis was totally beyond his comprehension. In spite of the refusal the two men had become friends.

'Take your problem to Racine,' Froissart concluded, 'for if any man can solve it, he can.'

'Many thanks for your suggestion.'

They switched their conversation from mathematics to the more mundane subject of foreign relations. The Entente Cordiale between France and England, signed less than two years previously, was by no means universally popular with the French. Anglophobes were furious with the Government for allying their country to its oldest enemy, and even those who understood the political necessity for France to acquire a reliable friend in face of the growing strength of Germany were cynical of the Entente's chances of survival.

'Even if nothing else undermines the Entente, Loubet will destroy it with his megalomania.'

Froissart's remark was intended as a joke. Loubet, who had been President of the Republic since 1899, was a mild, inoffensive man, more noted for his thriftiness and for the frumpish clothes of his wife than for any spectacular achievements in international diplomacy. The people despised him in a good-natured kind of way, throwing dung at him from time to time when he appeared in public. In spite of that, Loubet seemed likely to become the first president since the Third Republic was formed to finish his seven-year term of office in the manner prescribed by the constitution. His predecessors had all either been forced to resign, resigned in pique, died in the arms of a naked mistress or been assassinated.

Presently the other members of their little group arrived to join Gautier and Froissart. The deputy from Val-de-Marne was the first, and he was followed by Duthrey, who had a companion, a fellow journalist from *Figaro*, whom he introduced as Marcel Vettard. Vettard was a small, rotund man, not unlike Duthrey in build and elegantly dressed in top hat, frock coat, patent leather boots and kid gloves. His eyes were lively and his tongue quick.

'Monsieur Vettard reports on sport for our paper,' Duthrey explained, 'and particularly on horse-racing. He is acknowledged as the greatest expert on the Turf in France.'

'You exaggerate, dear friend.'

'If you know so much about bloodstock and racing form, you must be a wealthy man,' Froissart told him.

'Not at all. I know too much about horses to bet anything more than a few francs on them. Horses are like women. The better bred they are, the more unpredictably they behave.'

'Are you implying,' Gautier asked Vettard, 'that a man who knows too much about women should avoid them?'

'Certainly not! He may enjoy their company, pursue them, even adore them, but he should never lavish extravagant gifts on them. Like horses, they are a poor investment.'

'Are you going to Longchamp?' the deputy asked. There was a race meeting at Longchamp in the Bois de Boulogne that afternoon.

'Yes. I shall be going there directly from here.'

'Can you give us a tip?'

'My advice to you is to keep your money, but if you insist on having a gamble, try Whitebait in the fourth race.'

'What a splendid life!' Froissart exclaimed. 'An afternoon at Longchamp. All expenses paid by your newspaper, I assume.'

'Certainly,' Vettard replied. 'And it so happens that I have an extra complimentary ticket for this afternoon. Would one of you gentlemen care to accompany me?' No one seemed inclined to take up his offer, so he went on, 'Of course, it will not be one of the great occasions as in the days when the Prince of Wales used to come, surrounded by lovely ladies.'

'One hears that he still has mistresses, even though now he is a king,' Duthrey said disapprovingly.

'On the other hand, the President of the Republic has agreed to honour us with his presence.'

'In that case, one assumes gentlemen will not be allowed to carry canes.'

Everybody laughed. The deputy was alluding to an occasion some time previously when, during the Grand Prix at Longchamp, a Baron Christian, wearing the white carnation of the royalists, had lost his temper with Loubet and struck him on the top hat with his cane in the presidential box.

As he listened to the conversation, Gautier felt suddenly uneasy. The President was on the list of Condemned Ones and there would be few better places for an assassin to strike than at a race meeting. No matter how many policemen might be in attendance, and how closely they guarded Loubet, it would be easy for the murderer to fire a shot or throw a bomb and then vanish into the huge crowds.

'May I accept your offer, Monsieur?' he asked Vettard, 'and come with you to Longchamp?'

Gautier had never been to horse-racing before, for he had always believed that the sport would not interest him, but that afternoon he soon understood why it appealed to people from all levels of society. Longchamp provided a pageant of colour and ceremonial and noise: colour in the grandstand where convention allowed ladies, in the spectacular creations of their couturiers and modistes, to wear colours which they would never wear by day in the city; ceremonial in the parade of horses before the race, their mounting by the jockeys, their leisurely canter down to the start; noise in the hum of the crowd turning to the roar of cheers as the horses' hooves thundered past in the last few metres of a race. And behind the colour and the ceremonial and the noise was excitement – not just the expectancy and tension over the outcome of each race, but a continuing, vibrant excitement, the enjoyment of a great spectacle.

Their complimentary tickets, Vettard told Gautier, allowed them to go anywhere on the racecourse, the grandstand, the enclosures, the parade ring, anywhere except the private boxes in which the wealthy would entertain their friends and watch the racing in comfort. Moreover, as racing correspondent of *Figaro*, he would be welcome in the boxes of most of the owners of racehorses which would be running that day. They had arrived in good time, well before the first race was due to start, and he took Gautier everywhere, stopping to talk to trainers and jockeys and even stable lads, to anyone who might know a reason why a horse might perform exceptionally well or exceptionally badly that afternoon. When they were in the vicinity of the presidential box, Gautier was reassured to see the large number of police on hand. The box itself was empty then, but it would have been thoroughly searched for any bombs that might have been hidden there.

Loubet was late in arriving and Gautier began to wonder whether cowardice had proved stronger than a sense of duty and the President had abandoned his visit to the races. Eventually he appeared in the state carriage accompanied by his wife and entourage, and their arrival provoked nothing more dramatic than a little tepid applause from the spectators.

The first two races of the afternoon were both closely fought, with several horses contesting the finish and the eventual winner getting past the post first with less than a length to spare. Gautier and Vettard watched them from a special box provided for newspaper reporters. In the interval between the second and third races, Vettard suggested that they should visit the private box where the actor Jules Durey was entertaining a group of friends.

'Durey has a horse running in the fourth race this afternoon,' Vettard explained, 'which is likely to be the favourite and I would like to discuss its chances of winning with him.'

'Are you sure he will not mind my accompanying you?'

'I know he won't. He is a most sociable fellow who loves to be surrounded by friends. And he's very free with his champagne.'

Jules Durey was one of the leading actors in France, as highly regarded by the critics as Coquelin *aîné* and Guitry and equally at home in tragedy and comedy. Acting had become a respectable profession only in the last thirty or forty years. Before that, actors had been no more than interpreters for the sombre dramas and comedies written by teams of hack playwrights. Theatres put on new plays three or four times a month, actors rehearsed and performed continuously throughout the year, and for society going to the theatre was little more than a pretext for supper *en ville* afterwards. Now things were changing. Plays were written as vehicles for the best actors and actresses and Jules Durey could afford to own race-horses, a yacht and an automobile and to entertain leading personalities from *le monde*.

He welcomed Vettard and Gautier effusively and began telling them how well his horse had performed in training. The horse had been named, appropriately, 'Curtain Call', and Vettard told Durey he was confident that it would win its race, although earlier at the Café Corneille he had given Gautier's friends a different tip. As they were talking, Gautier glanced round the box and was surprised to see Michelle Le Tellier among the guests.

When he went over to her she seemed embarrassed. 'Monsieur Gautier! I did not know you were a devotee of horse-racing.'

'This is my first visit to a racecourse. And you Madame?' Gautier replied. The fact that even though she had smiled agreeably she had not called him by his christian name was meant to signify something, Gautier supposed, but he did not know what.

'My husband used to bring me sometimes. He was fond of gambling. I come because I love horses and, of course, to see my friends. And speaking of friends, did you know that Princesse Sophia is here this afternoon?'

'I did not, no.'

'Oh, yes. She is in the box of Monsieur Weill, the banker. People tell me she is an incorrigible gambler.'

'Why not, if she can afford it?'

107

'But can she?'

'Have you seen anyone else of note here?' Gautier tried to keep the irritation he felt out of his voice. This was the second occasion when Michelle had made disparaging comments about Princesse Sophia and he could see no reason for it. A vainer man might have thought it simply jealousy, but he knew that Michelle had never been jealous of her husband's mistresses nor possessive enough to quarrel over his many infidelities. Moreover, in this case she had no cause to be jealous.

'Jacques Mounet is here. We met him at Madame Mauberge's soirée, remember?'

'Yes, I remember.' Gautier thought it prudent not to tell Michelle of the circumstances under which he had met Mounet twice since the soirée.

'Have you read any of his books?'

'Only one. *Seraglio*.'

'That's the one I like least.' Michelle wrinkled her nose in disdain. 'It's too erotic and the story is far-fetched.'

'I thought it was based on his own experiences.'

'That's what he would like us to think, but I suspect that his very vivid imagination played a greater role in it. You should read *Requiem*. That's his latest book and in my opinion his best.'

Mounet's latest book, Michelle told Gautier, was the story of a young Breton whose father had served and died under Napoleon and who was brought up by his mother in poverty. The boy had become a fisherman, enduring great hardships and danger to support the family. After years he had succeeded, saving enough money to buy a fishing boat of his own, then two, then a fleet of boats. But success had come too late and his mother, whom he adored, had died, worn out by work and suffering, before she could enjoy the comforts and luxuries he was able to buy her.

'The story is profoundly moving,' Michelle concluded. 'And it's largely autobiographical. Jacques too worshipped his mother, although of course it was not the trials and dangers of a fisherman's life that brought him wealth and fame.'

As Michelle was finishing what she was saying, her attention appeared to be distracted and Gautier realised that she was looking past him. She said, abruptly, 'Admiral Pottier is my escort this afternoon.'

'I didn't see him here when I arrived.'

'He has been to see the horses in the parade ring and has just returned.'

Looking round, Gautier saw Pottier coming towards them. When he saw Gautier he bowed his head slightly as an acknowledgement, but stiffly. He took Michelle's hand in his.

'My dear, I hope Inspecteur Gautier has told you how ravishing you look this afternoon.'

'He has not come to Longchamp to pay compliments, I am sure.'

'You are not on police business, surely, Inspecteur.'

'No, Monsieur.'

'I am delighted to hear it. Our host insists that we enjoy ourselves.'

Pottier nodded in the direction of Jules Durey. The three of them chatted for a time, sipping the Mumm champagne which a waiter brought them. Pottier was in a friendly mood and appeared to have forgotten or at least forgiven the rebuff that Gautier had given him in the Cercle St Honoré. The man's changing moods, Gautier decided, could be a sign of an unstable personality, the result perhaps of the disappointment he had suffered in his political career and frustrated ambition.

When the third race of the afternoon had been run, Gautier and Vettard left the box. The fourth race was the most important of the meeting, carrying easily the richest prize, and one could sense the mounting expectation of the crowds as the runners were brought into the parade ring.

Vettard told Gautier that he was going to place a bet.

'On Whitebait? Or Curtain Call?'

Vettard grinned. 'Neither. I have confidential information that another horse will win, which I have kept to myself so that the odds against it will not fall. Would you like me to wager something on it for you as well?'

'No, but you could put twenty-five francs on number nine for me.'

'Number nine? The filly Edith? She has no form at all.'

'Even so.'

As Vettard went off to place the bets, Gautier smiled. His decision to have a bet was no more than a sudden impulse, based on a feeling that having come to a race meeting he should sample the excitement it had to offer, in however small a way. If anyone knew how he made his choice of a horse to bet on, they would have mocked him. In his apartment the previous evening he had once again taken his pack of cards, pulled out those that had been shown against the names of the Condemned Ones and studied them, looking for some sequence of numbers that might give him a clue to the role they played in the plot. Once again he had found nothing except that when he added up the number of pips on each of the cards, he found he had a total of sixty-three. If one added the two digits of that number together one had the figure nine, and he had noticed that there was no card higher than nine shown on the list. The number seven, he had heard, was thought by ancient philosophers to have a magical significance, and if one divided sixty-three by seven, once again one had nine. As a basis for betting on a horse it was ludicrous, but for someone as ignorant as he was of horses and racing form it was good enough.

Left on his own, he strolled around the parade ring, past other enclosures and then along the front of the grandstand. The horses running in the fourth race would be going down to the start in a few minutes and already people were moving forward to the rails from where they would get a better view of the finish. He recalled seeing a painting of racing during the Grand Prix at Longchamp by Béraud, one of the popular artists of the day. Béraud had captured the stylish elegance of the occasion, but not the animation, the flushed faces, the excitement.

As he was passing one of the entrances which led to the upper tiers of the grandstand, he heard screams coming from the direction of a mob of people who were clustered in a tight circle, jostling to get a better view of whatever was happening in the centre. The screams had come from a woman and now other voices began shouting.

'Help! Murder! Fetch a doctor! The police! Quick!'

Quickly Gautier fought his way through the crowd, elbowing people aside and calling out that he was from the police. Reluctantly, not wishing to miss the sensation, they let him through.

A stout man was lying in a heap in the centre of the crowd of onlookers, unconscious if he was not already dead. His top hat had been knocked off and his hand was pressed against a wound in his left side from which blood had gushed, staining his waistcoat and glove and gathering in a pool on the ground beside him. A woman in a blue dress was kneeling over the man, with her back towards Gautier, holding his other hand and trying to revive him by patting his cheek. Gently but firmly Gautier pushed her to one side as he bent down and reached for the man's heart to see whether he was still alive. When she turned to look at him, he saw that it was Princesse Sophia Dashkova. She was pale and anxious, but did not seem surprised to see him.

'Who is he?' she asked, nodding towards the man on the ground.

'The Minister of Finance, Louis Risson-Vernet.'

'Is he dead?'

'No. Unconscious and shocked I should say.'

'I have smelling salts in my reticule.'

111

Princesse Sophia took a small bottle of smelling salts from her purse and handed it to Gautier. They were not needed, for at that moment Risson-Vernet's eyelids began to flutter and presently he opened his eyes and groaned. He stared at Gautier uncomprehendingly.

'What's happened to me?' He grimaced with pain.

'You have been stabbed, Monsieur.'

'God in Heaven! Then it's true! Someone is trying to kill me!'

'Fortunately he has not succeeded. Stay where you are till medical help arrives.' Gautier turned to Princesse Sophia. 'Did you see what happened?'

'Not really. This gentleman was just in front of me as I was coming out of the grandstand. Then suddenly he gave a gasp and collapsed.'

'He has been knifed. Did you see who might have done it?'

Princesse Sophia shook her head. 'There were so many people around, it was a struggle just to get through.'

Gautier looked up at the people surrounding them who were standing staring at the wounded man, fascinated by the macabre drama that had been played in front of them. 'Did anyone see who attacked this gentleman?'

The onlookers shook their heads, except for one man who spoke up. 'A man rushed past immediately after it happened, pushing everyone out of his way.'

'Did you see him attack this gentleman? Did you see a knife in his hands?'

'No. As I say he was rushing away. A tall man he was, with a beard and long hair.'

Before Gautier could ask the man any more questions a doctor arrived. At race meetings at Longchamp there was always a doctor in attendance and a small ambulance team, although they were seldom required to do anything except revive the many women who fainted from excitement or in the heat. A stretcher was brought and Risson-Vernet was carried away to the medical room so that his wound could be treated and the flow of blood staunched before he was taken to hospital. Two policemen, who had been patrolling near the entrance to the grandstand as part of the precautions to protect the President, also arrived and with their help Gautier began questioning the people in the crowd to find out if anyone had seen anything which might help identify the Minister of Finance's attacker. He was not optimistic.

He had no more than begun when he heard cheering from the direction of the racecourse which told him that the fourth race of the afternoon was being run. Presently there was a great shout and frenzied applause.

'I wonder which horse won,' Princesse Sophia remarked.

'A rank outsider,' a man who had watched the finish of the race said gloomily. 'The filly Edith.'

10

That evening Gautier dined with Princesse Sophia again, but not tête-à-tête this time, nor in the centre of Paris. The princess had stayed with him at Longchamp throughout the time when he was questioning people about the attack on Risson-Vernet and had accompanied him when he went to the medical room to speak to the wounded man. Gautier was not sure why, for she had not been able to be of any help, and if, as one might assume, she had gone to the races with friends, one would have thought that she would have wished to rejoin them.

The last race had been run, the meeting was over and the crowds were drifting away before Gautier had finished all that had to be done. The Minister of Finance had been taken in an ambulance to hospital under police escort and Gautier had sent a policeman with a message telling Courtrand of the attempted assassination. When any incident involving a government minister or other person of importance occurred, the director-general had to be informed, no matter where he might be.

Only when Gautier was ready to leave Longchamp did Princesse Sophia say to him, 'I have invited a few friends to dine in the Pavillon d'Armenonville this evening. Would you care to join us?' Gautier must have shown his surprise at such an unconventional invitation, for she smiled. 'I must be honest and tell you that one of my guests has let me down and the party needs another man.'

'I would have to go home and change.'

'That is not a problem. We are not dining early. I am going to Paris myself first.'

The Pavillon d'Armenonville was in the Bois de Boulogne not far from Longchamp, and although he had never been there, Gautier knew that it had the reputation of being one of the finest and most elegant restaurants in Paris. When he was still Prince of Wales, Edward VII often dined there after going racing at Longchamp, usually in the company of the beautiful young French lady who happened to be his favourite mistress at the time.

An open Victoria carriage with its coachman in livery was waiting for the princess, and Gautier drove back into the city with her. On the way she explained that she was giving the dinner party that night to repay some of the hospitality she had received since arriving in Paris. Monsieur and Madame Mauberge, in whose home Gautier and she had met, would be among the guests, and so would Jules Durey and his wife. When Gautier told her that he had been in the actor's box at the races that afternoon, the princess explained that Durey had invited her there as well but she had already accepted an invitation from another friend, Monsieur Weill the banker. As he listened to her, Gautier found himself wondering whether her real reason for refusing Durey's invitation might not have been that she knew Michelle Le Tellier would be there. He had sensed a coldness between the two women which could easily turn into hostility.

Later, when they gathered in the Pavillon d'Armenonville, he found that there would be ten at dinner. In addition to those the princess had already named there were two more couples: the banker Edmond Weill and his wife, and a playwright, Victor Caplet, with his actress wife Fiona. Gautier was never told the name of the man whose place he had been invited to fill.

Although he was not usually impressed by wealth, nor by the luxury and expensive possessions which symbolised

115

it, he could not help admiring the Pavillon d'Armenonville, with its high ceiling supported by marble columns, its chandeliers and the glass doors which separated the dining room from the trees and grass of the Bois de Boulogne and which in summer would be drawn back. That evening it was as animated as Longchamp had been in the afternoon, but in a more relaxed and sophisticated style, bright with the noise of conversation and laughter and with the colour of the ladies' dresses vivid against the black and white formality of the men, the white of tablecloths and napkins, the silver of the cutlery.

The women were wearing hats too, which they would never do dining at night *en ville*. The mode that season was for large straw hats decorated with artificial flowers or fruit, muslin roses surrounded by marguerites, clusters of cherries or grapes or apples. Some even had imitation birds perched among the flowers, but ostrich feathers, which had been all the vogue not long ago, were now scorned. Surrounded by reminders of the orchard and the garden and looking out into the *bois*, one had the feeling of dining in the country, a sumptuous and opulent picnic.

In parallel with Gautier's thoughts, the conversation at table turned quite early to women's dress. Durey and Caplet began to mock the prevailing fashions.

'When a woman passes,' Durey said, 'one sees only a movement of material, a displacement of silk, satin, velvet, lace; skirts pleated and gathered with underskirts to fill them out; corsages and collars and sleeves and of course gloves; veils as well often, so one gets not a glimpse of the woman herself.'

'You're right,' Caplet agreed. 'Women glide past like majestic ships in full sail.'

'Even hands are covered with muffs. A woman's clothes are designed to conceal her body and so to titillate the imagination of the poor, frustrated man.'

'Poor males indeed!' Madame Mauberge exclaimed. 'If

a woman so much as takes off a glove or the pin out of her hat, men imagine that they are being encouraged and grow insupportably bold.'

'Frenchmen should consider themselves fortunate,' Princesse Sophia said. 'In my country all you would see of a woman would be her eyes. Much of the time they would see nothing, for women are kept behind locked doors.'

'In a harem?' Madame Weill asked her. 'Is that really true?'

'Regrettably, yes. It's a barbaric custom.'

'Tell us about your plans for next year, my dear,' Monsieur Mauberge said. He may have thought that the harem was not a suitable topic for conversation in front of ladies.

'Next year the princess will definitely be back in Paris with an opera company,' Monsieur Weill said. 'You can count on that. And it will include singers better than Ivan Grigov.'

'Monsieur Weill was one of my backers this year,' Princesse Sophia explained to the others.

'And I will be again next year.'

'One hopes that you did not all lose too heavily by the cancellation of this year's tour,' Gautier remarked.

'Not at all. No tickets had been sold and the theatres in which the company was due to perform were able to obtain other bookings. Our commitments were trifling.'

'You and my other backers were very understanding and kind. No one complained.'

'Except Fleury,' Monsieur Weill said. 'The man's a bounder.'

'Fleury?'

'Yes, Adolph Fleury,' Durey said. 'He is a money-lender who has aspirations to be an impresario.'

'Now that the theatre has become so popular,' Caplet complained, 'everyone wants to make money by exploiting the talents of actors and playwrights.'

117

'That's rather unfair,' Princesse Sophia said. 'Someone has to provide the money to put on a play and the backer should surely be entitled to a profit.'

They began talking about the stage, about the unpredictability of audiences and the self-importance of critics who had the power to bring any new production to an end merely on a whim. From plays and producers the conversation veered inevitably to actors and actresses. Fiona Caplet was considered by many to be the finest of the younger actresses in France. She was beautiful, and partly Scottish by birth, which must have explained her red hair, very fair skin and hazel eyes. Seeing her for the first time at close range, Gautier was struck by how small and slight she was, but people who had seen her in her husband's latest drama, *Josephine*, said that she dominated the stage with her commanding presence and superbly modulated voice.

'You are the future of the French theatre,' her husband told Fiona. 'Within two years you will be better known abroad than Sarah Bernhardt.'

'You exaggerate, *chéri*.'

'Why not? You're a better actress than she.'

'Not better than the great Sarah, surely?' Madame Weill was one of the older generation who still revered Sarah Bernhardt in the closing days of her career.

'Certainly,' Durey said firmly. 'I never saw Bernhardt act when she was young, but her performance now is farcical; all ranting and grimacing, worse than the worst melodrama.'

Sarah Bernhardt had been accepted for many years as the greatest actress in France and, with the possible exception of Eleanora Duse, in the world, She had toured America triumphantly several times, been received by royalty all over Europe and survived the notoriety of many scandals. Now she was over sixty. Dramatists no longer wrote plays for her, and she appeared only in tired repetitions of the great roles of her youth, *La Dame aux camélias* and *Fédora*, with second-rate actors.

'What about Simone Suffren?' Princesse Sophia asked. 'One hears flattering reports of her acting.'

'Suffren!' Durey exclaimed. 'She was a pretty little *midinette*, nothing more, until Bonnat painted her in a ballet skirt. Ziddler then put her in a grotesque pantomime at the Moulin Rouge and the next thing is we are expected to believe she is an actress.'

'She is dressed by Paquin,' Fiona Caplet remarked.

'And undressed by princes, grand dukes and millionaires,' Gautier put in. He had heard of the many love affairs of Simone Suffren.

'Lucky girl,' Madame Mauberge said wistfully. She liked making remarks which she hoped would shock people, but usually shocked only her husband.

After dinner Gautier was driven back to the city in Princesse Sophia's other carriage, not an open Victoria this time but a *calèche* with its hood pulled up. Sitting next to the princess in the darkness, he was aware of her presence and of her perfume, gardenia he thought it was, but could not be sure. When the *calèche* was rattling along a cobbled street, she was thrown against him and he felt her shoulder and hips against his. The contact was brief but he realised that she could easily arouse him.

'How well do you know Monsieur Fleury?' he asked her.

'The financier?'

'Yes. Why? Are there two?'

'I believe so. The financier has a cousin who is an author.'

'I was thinking of the financier.'

'I hardly know him at all. Monsieur Weill arranged a consortium of backers for my opera tour and Fleury was one of them.'

'Did I understand that he was proving difficult?'

'Difficult?' The princess replied. 'That's an understatement. He wanted to sue me, although it was through no fault of mine that the tour had to be cancelled. Then, when the other backers refused to join him, he started making libellous statements about me.'

Gautier would have liked to ask her if she could explain why the names Fleury and Grigov had been on the list of Condemned Ones, but the Sûreté was still keeping the list secret, although with increasing difficulty as the reports of murders and attacks increased. The newspapers were asking questions and were not satisfied with the answers they were being given.

When they reached her house in rue Jacob, she invited him in to take a glass of cognac. A Frenchwoman living alone would never have made such an invitation to a man she scarcely knew, but Gautier supposed that living and travelling in different countries had given the princess a cosmopolitan and more liberal attitude. He accepted the invitation and found that the princess's maid had left in the drawing room not only a decanter of cognac and glasses but cigars in a silver box. Before pouring the cognac, the princess took off her gloves and hat and, with what resembled a sigh, unpinned her hair as well, allowing it to fall to her shoulders.

'Aren't you taking a risk?' Gautier teased her. 'As Madame Mauberge said at dinner, a man might take that as encouragement.'

'You may interpret it as you wish,' Princesse Sophia said, and her smile was impossible to interpret.

When they were sitting facing each other with a glass of cognac in their hands, Gautier asked her, 'The maid whom I met when I was last here was named Marie-Ann, was she not?'

'Yes. She is my personal maid.'

'Is she the girl who was to marry the Comte de Neuville's footman?'

'No, she is another of my maids. Wasn't that a dreadful accident?'

'I am not convinced it was an accident.'

'It could not have been intentional, surely? Who would wish to kill that poor man?'

Any answer that Gautier might have given to her question would have been no more than speculation, so he shrugged his shoulders. They began to talk about the dinner party at the Pavillon d'Armenonville. The princess thanked him again for agreeing to make up the numbers, but she still did not tell him whose place he had taken. Recalling the remark that had been made about the actress Simone Suffren, she asked him about the reference to the painter Bonnat. Gautier told her that Léon Bonnat was one of the most successful portrait painters in France. He was one of the old school of classical artists, the *'pompiers'* as the disciples of the new impressionist school derisively called them, but his prestige was so great that he was able to charge 40,000 francs and even more for a portrait. People said that if a businessman about to go bankrupt announced that Bonnat was painting his portrait, his credit would immediately be restored. Gautier knew something about the subject, not because he had ever taken a deep interest in art, but because he had once investigated the murder in Montmartre of an art dealer.

'Talking of paintings,' he said, 'I keep looking at that miniature on your mantelpiece. It's exquisite.'

'Isn't it?'

The miniature was a portrait of a girl of perhaps fifteen, showing no more than her head and shoulders. She was beautiful, and Gautier had a vague feeling that he had seen her somewhere before. 'Who is the girl?'

'A cousin of mine, a very dear cousin,' the princess replied after a slight hesitation. 'She is dead, poor creature.'

The sadness in the princess's expression as she answered was so poignant that Gautier wished he had not asked the question. He realised that he had intruded on a private grief and quickly changed the subject, returning once again to talking about the dinner party at the Pavillon d'Armenonville.

When he heard a clock chime two and stood up to leave, Princesse Sophia said, 'Must you go?'

She was an attractive woman who, late at night and after the wine and brandy he had drunk, seemed even more seductive. In other circumstances Gautier would have stayed to find out how much he should read into her question, but there were times when checks and restraints held him back. This was one of those occasions.

'I must, I am afraid,' he replied. 'I have an early start tomorrow.'

She smiled as he kissed her hand and seemed amused. As he was walking along rue Jacob heading for his apartment, he thought again about the miniature on the mantelpiece, trying to visualise the face, trying to recall when he might have seen it before. Suddenly he remembered. The face was the face of the young girl whose portrait he had seen on the easel in Jacques Mounet's apartment.

11

Next morning Surat was waiting for him when he arrived at the Sûreté, to report on the enquiries that had been made the previous day. The first report was negative, for Surat had learnt nothing about the Russian bass Grigov that would explain why he should be a target for assassination. He was a singer of international reputation, highly regarded in his profession, married and with three children. There was no hint of domestic problems nor of any scandal in his life. The singers in the chorus and other lesser performers at l'Opéra, where he was appearing, spoke of his quick and violent temper, which was matched by moodiness and displays of temperament, but these were accepted as the prerogative of a famous singer.

Surat's second report was more interesting. A rowing boat stolen from a small boatyard in the Port des Invalides, not far from the Chambre des Députés, had been found abandoned below Pont St-Louis behind Notre Dame. The boat had been missing since the morning of the explosion on Valanis's houseboat and its description matched that of the one Gautier had seen being rowed away from the houseboat.

'Now at least we know exactly how the bomb was taken to the houseboat,' Gautier said.

'He must be a very determined man to row all that way. It must be all of three kilometres.'

'To establish who it was will be more difficult. We have to assume that he knew there were boats moored at the Port des Invalides. No one would go out at night on the

123

off-chance of finding one somewhere. so it will be someone who either knows the area well or had reconnoitred it. Go to the boatyard and ask around the people there if they noticed anyone taking an unusual interest in the boats or behaving in any way abnormally during the few days prior to the explosion.'

While they were talking a messenger came into the room with an envelope which, he explained, had just been left at the Sûreté for the inspector. When Gautier opened it he found 450 francs in banknotes with a visiting card pinned to them. The card was that of Marcel Vettard and on the back he had scribbled:

Monsieur Gautier – when I collected your winnings at Longchamp I could not find you to hand them over to. Congratulations! You should be doing my job!

In the confusion caused by the attack on Risson-Vernet, Gautier had forgotten the bet which he asked Vettard to place for him. Surat was watching as he unpinned the visiting card from the notes and counted them. Four hundred and fifty francs would seem a considerable sum to a policeman of Surat's rank, far more than he earned in a month.

'This is not a bribe,' Gautier told him, smiling.

'I never imagined that it was,' Surat replied, looking shocked.

'For the first and probably the last time in my life I bet on a horse.' Gautier took a hundred francs from the wad of notes and held it out to Surat. 'Here, buy your wife some flowers and take her out to dinner.'

'I couldn't possibly accept it, *patron*.'

'I have no one else with whom to celebrate my luck. Ask your wife if she will do me the honour. Besides, old friend, you have been working too many evenings recently. We both owe your wife and your children a little treat.'

After Surat had left, Gautier looked through the reports of the other inspectors working on the case. All of them had been busy, but to little effect, and no evidence had been found of any association between Astrux and Ribot, nor to show that Astrux had left his home in the early hours of the morning when the bomb exploded on the houseboat. Ribot himself had been questioned again by the *juge d'instruction* for several hours, but his story that he had been given the package to take into the law courts could not be shaken. Gautier found only one item among all the reports which had been placed on his desk that caught his interest. The medical experts who had carried out an autopsy on the Comte de Neuville's footman were reasonably satisfied that they had identified the poison which had killed the man. That in itself was an achievement, for little was known about poisons, and murders by poison often went unsolved for that reason. What interested Gautier even more was that the quantity of the poison, belladonna, which the footman had inadvertently taken would not in the normal way have been enough to kill a healthy man. The footman, unknown to himself or his employer, had been suffering from an obscure weakness of the heart, and that was the reason why the dose had proved fatal.

Soon after nine o'clock a message arrived that the senior inspectors were assembling for the morning meeting. Gautier guessed that for Courtrand to be at the Sûreté and ready for work so early would mean trouble for everyone, and he was right. The director-general was in a rage and when Gautier reached his office he was shouting at his secretary. When he saw Gautier he began shouting at him instead.

'And you, Gautier! Have you any idea how much trouble I was caused yesterday evening?'

'Monsieur?'

'My wife and I were dining with the First Secretary of

the British Embassy. The evening was ruined. My wife had to go to dinner without me and I could only join her later. They had to delay the first course of the meal on my account.'

'Did you not wish to be informed of the attempt on the minister's life?'

'Of course, but I had to go to the hospital and was kept waiting for almost an hour before I was allowed to speak to him.'

'I agree that it would have been more convenient if he could have been stabbed earlier in the afternoon.'

Courtrand was too agitated to appreciate Gautier's gentle sarcasm. He went on, 'And what, may I ask, were you doing at Longchamp?'

'The President was there and I was afraid that there might be an attack on his life.'

'The President, the Minister of Finance, how many others were there I wonder. How do these people expect me to protect them?'

When the inspectors had all arrived the meeting began with a discussion of the stabbing at Longchamp. Gautier explained that the people who had been close to Risson–Vernet when he was stabbed could give only a confused account of what had happened. And Risson–Vernet had been too shocked to remember anything.

'When I saw him in hospital,' Courtrand said, 'some fragments of his memory had returned. He recalls that he was coming out of the grandstand on his way to join his wife who was with friends in one of the enclosures. Suddenly he felt an agonising pain in his side and he must have fainted, although he does not remember falling.'

'Does he remember nothing more?' one of the inspectors asked.

'Nothing clearly. There was a throng of people near the exit from the grandstand, some going one way, some the other. The minister believes there was a woman coming

126

towards him, for he has the impression that he was struck by her beauty.'

'He says she was coming towards him?' Gautier asked. 'Is he certain of that?'

'He is not certain of anything. The doctor thinks that the position and direction of the knife wound indicate that he was stabbed by someone coming towards him and on his left. As I see it, the attacker must have been aiming for his heart, but fortunately he missed and the wound is not grave.'

'That suggests that whoever it was meant to stab the minister and hurry on past him. In the press of people around them no one would notice.'

'And no one did.'

'In that case the assailant must be left-handed,' Gautier said.

'What of it?' Courtrand asked.

'The two men murdered in Pigalle appear to have been stabbed by a right-handed person.'

'Which supports my original view that the whole plot is the work of a group of people, anarchists, no doubt.'

They discussed the other reports of the previous day's investigations and the inspectors put forward theories, but without any real conviction. Gautier could sense a general depression, a feeling that while they had not yet reached an impasse, no progress was being made and that they were powerless to stop the murders continuing. Eventually Courtrand decided to bring the meeting to an end.

'Messieurs, have any of you further comments or suggestions?'

'One thing strikes me as odd,' Gautier remarked.

'What's that?'

'The person or people responsible for these attacks appears to be remarkably incompetent. After the first four murders, we have had a bomb which exploded without killing anyone, a stabbing which failed and poison which

127

was swallowed by the wrong victim. And if we assume that the poison was intended for Madame Dubois, the Comte de Neuville's cook, the amount she would have taken would probably not have been enough to kill her.'

'Then we should count ourselves fortunate that they are incompetent,' Courtrand said.

Leaving the office of the director-general, the inspectors went to their own offices which were all on higher floors of the building and all decorated and furnished in the dismal colours and style to be found in government offices. Gautier had no sooner reached his room when a message arrived saying that he was wanted again by Courtrand.

'I have just had a telephone call from Monsieur Jacques Mounet,' Courtrand told him. 'He was very agitated.'

'Why? Not another poisoning, surely?'

'No. His servant Yussif has disappeared. You had better get over to his apartment at once. We cannot rule out the possibility that this is part of a plot against him.'

Gautier left at once for rue Murillo, but not with any sense of urgency. The morning was warm and sunny and he decided to ride on one of the old horse-drawn omnibuses, a leisurely experience which would not be there to enjoy for much longer, now that the motor buses were coming into service. He had formed the impression that Jacques Mounet was an excitable man who liked and expected instant attention, and he did not believe that his life was in any imminent danger.

Mounet was waiting for him, dressed in robes which Gautier thought to be of Persian origin, not in one of his fantasy rooms but in a study where, one supposed, he did his writing, for there were quill pens, ink and blotting paper on the table together with at least a ream of pink paper. According to reports in the newspapers Mounet always wrote on pink paper. Occupying a central place in the bookcase were several volumes bound in pale blue leather which, Gautier supposed, must be his own novels.

A fine, jewelled sword presented to him by the Sultan of Turkey hung on one wall among many other mementoes of his travels.

'Yussif has disappeared!' Mounet seemed distraught.

'So I have been told. When did you last see him?'

'The night before last. Since you told me that my life might be in danger, he has insisted on sleeping on a mattress outside the door to my bedroom. When one of my other servants came to wake me yesterday morning, Yussif was not there.'

'Did anyone in the house see him leave?'

'No. He must have left at first dawn.'

'And you have no idea where he might have gone?'

Mounet hesitated. 'Not really. He did say the previous day that he might go and buy a pistol, so that he could protect me properly. We have no firearms in the apartment, only an old naval cutlass.'

'Where is his home?' Gautier did not consider it very likely that anyone would go out to buy a pistol at dawn.

'In Brittany.'

'Might he not have gone there?'

'Not without asking me. Yussif is much more than servant to me, Inspecteur. I have always treated him like a brother and he is devoted to me.'

There were other questions which Gautier would have liked to have asked Mounet, but he did not think that this was the time for them. So he took out his notebook. 'We will begin a search for Yussif at once, Monsieur. First, may I have his full name?'

'Lucien Desmarais.'

'I wish I had known that before.'

'Why?'

'Desmarais is one of the names on the list of which I told you.'

*

129

Professor Racine had his study on the top floor of a very old building in the university quarter. He was a tall man with a bony face, who carried a monocle and pince-nez, both suspended from his neck on ribbon, and used them indiscriminately. His study was a chaos of sheets of paper covered in figures, on his desk and the chairs and piles of books on the carpet and even in the fireplace. Along the full length of one wall was a blackboard covered in numbers and equations. He threw some papers off a chair so that Gautier could have a place to sit.

'I apologise for all this,' he said, waving at the room around him. 'No doubt you dislike untidiness as much as I do.'

'With so many papers and books it must be difficult to keep a room tidy.'

'I could do it if I wished. You should see our home – as neat and well arranged as a hospital ward. My wife is untidy and I follow her around the house tidying up after her. The disorder here is deliberate. My students expect it from a professor, you understand. If the room were well ordered, they would begin to doubt my intellect.'

Realising that he was in the presence of one of Paris's many eccentrics, Gautier decided he was going to enjoy his visit. 'Monsieur Froissart suggested that I should come to you for advice.'

'Froissart? A noble man but no mathematician. He considers my book is not good enough to publish.'

'Perhaps that is because he finds it too difficult to understand,' Gautier replied tactfully. 'He speaks very highly of your mathematical ability.'

'My calculating ability, you mean.'

'Are they not the same?'

'Not at all. I could calculate before I could talk.'

'That isn't possible, surely?' Gautier asked incredulously.

Racine smiled his shy smile. 'I cannot prove it, of course, but I believe so. One thing I do know. I could calculate before I had been taught any arithmetic. Let me tell you a story.'

Racine told Gautier that his father had been a veterinary surgeon in Rennes. One evening when Racine was not yet three years old, his father and mother were trying to reckon up the income earned in the practice during the past month. Racine's mother had a sheaf of bills and was calling out the amount of each in francs to his father, who wrote them down, more than fifty different figures in all. She had just called out the last number when Racine, who had been playing with his toys in the room, called out the total before his father had even begun to add the numbers. His parents had checked the boy's answer and had been astonished to find it was correct.

'It seems scarcely possible,' Gautier commented.

'Not really. Let me show you.' The professor went over to his blackboard. He had no cloth to wipe it clean, so he cleared a space on it using the sleeve of his jacket. 'Give me a number of nine digits.'

Gautier called out a number, choosing the digits at random, and Racine wrote it on the blackboard, followed by a multiplication sign. 'Now another number, also of nine digits.'

Gautier called out another number. The professor wrote it down and, as soon as he had finished, without any pause for thought, began writing below it the product of the multiplication sum, from left to right, as though he already knew the answer. The whole demonstration could not have taken more than two minutes.

'There.' Racine grinned as he turned to face Gautier. 'Do you wish to check my calculation?'

'Thank you, no.' Gautier was astounded. 'It would take me until the evening. I believe you.'

'Of course, this isn't as difficult as it looks,' Racine said, rubbing his hands together to get rid of the chalk. 'There are short cuts in calculations of that type. For example,

131

I know the multiplication tables up to one hundred by heart.'

'Even so, it's amazing.'

'Some of the calculators who appear on the stage professionally do feats far more prodigious and spectacular than any I could show you.'

They began discussing the careers of some of the best known stage lightning calculators, the Englishman George Bidder, the Greek Pericles Diamandi and the Italian prodigy Jacques Inaudi. A committee had been formed by the Académie des Sciences to investigate the mental processes of Diamandi and Inaudi and Racine told Gautier that if he was interested in the subject he should read a book written by Alfred Binet, a member of that committee, on the psychology of calculators and chess-players.

'However, Inspecteur,' Racine said, 'you came to me for advice, you said, not for a chat on calculating. What is your problem?'

'It is a police matter, so I must ask you to treat it in confidence.'

'I understand.'

'I am not sure whether I should be seeking the advice of a mathematician or a poker player.'

'Mathematicians should make the best card-players, especially in games where chance is involved, but strangely very often they are the worst.'

Afraid that the professor was about to digress with a discourse on games of chance and the calculation of odds, Gautier quickly pulled out his copy of the list of Fifteen Condemned Ones. He explained to Racine the circumstances in which the list had been received by the Sûreté and that some of the people on it were already dead. He pointed out, too, that each name had a picture of a playing card drawn against it and that the cards were of different suits and different denominations.

'I wondered,' he concluded, 'whether the choice of card for each name might have some mathematical significance. For example, could the number of pips on a card indicate in some way the day of the week on which the person against whom it was shown would be murdered? Or is there a coded message in the sequence of the numbers?'

'An interesting possibility,' Racine remarked, looking down the list.

'Thinking it might help, I've brought a pack of cards with me.' Gautier took the pack from his pocket. 'And I have picked out the cards which were drawn against the names on the list.'

He placed the fifteen cards upwards on the desk. Clipping the pince-nez to his nose, Racine looked at the cards and then began pushing them about, haphazardly it seemed. His fingers were long and thin, with prominent knuckles, and he moved them stiffly as though his hands were artificial and powered by a mechanical device. After a minute or so he looked up at Gautier.

'You have studied these cards more than once, I am sure. Do you see anything about the choice of them which strikes you as significant?'

'There is no card higher than a nine.'

'Yes. Anything more?'

'The value of all the cards added together comes to sixty-three, and if one then adds the two digits of sixty-three together one has nine.'

'Excellent!' Racine said, as though he were encouraging a slow pupil who was at last beginning to make progress. 'Is that all?'

'One more thing, but it may not be significant. I was playing around with the cards, trying to see if I could find a sequence or pattern in their numbers, when I noticed that by placing five cards in a row, four above them, then three,

133

two and one, I could make a perfect triangle of fifteen cards.'

Racine appeared delighted. 'My dear Gautier, you are one of us. You have studied mathematics.'

'Only at a very elementary level.'

'Then that is a pity. You have a talent for mathematics.'

Gautier laughed. 'I wish that were true.'

'Believe me, it is. Some men are numerate, some are literate. You and I are numerate. I could explain my theory about that, and one day I will, but first we must deal with your problem. Have you heard of Pascal's triangle?'

When Gautier shook his head, Racine explained that Blaise Pascal, the seventeenth-century mathematician and philosopher, famous for his *Pensées*, an unfinished work on the Christian religion, and one of the greatest French prose writers, had also written a treatise on the arithmetic triangle. The triangle, although now generally described as Pascal's triangle, had however been known for centuries, was mentioned by Omar Khayyam in the twelfth century and was probably first discovered by the early Chinese philosophers.

'It's a fascinating pattern of numbers,' Racine said, 'so simple that a child could set it out and yet full of mathematical riches. Let me show you.'

Wiping another, larger area of the blackboard clean with his sleeve, he began writing down numbers in the pattern of a triangle. When he had finished, he stepped back so that Gautier could see it.

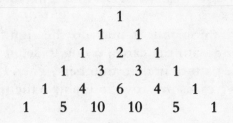

```
            1
          1   1
        1   2   1
      1   3   3   1
    1   4   6   4   1
  1   5   10  10  5   1
```

'You will see,' Racine told Gautier, 'that each number in the triangle is the sum of the two numbers immediately above it. Also that the sum of all the numbers in any row is twice the sum of the number in the row above it.'

'Yes. I see that.'

'The triangle has many uses, and one of its best-known applications is to probability theory.' Gautier's expression must have told Racine that he knew nothing of probability theory, for he went on, 'I will not bore you with an explanation. I'll just give you one example.'

Taking a stick of chalk, he wrote something against each row of numbers in his triangle. When he moved away Gautier could see what he had written.

			1				0 children
		1		1			1 child
	1		2		1		2 children
1		3		3		1	3 children

1		4		6		4		1	4 children
1	5		10		10		5	1	5 children

'Let us suppose that a married couple were planning to have a family and would like to know what the chances were of the children being boys or girls. If we read from the right-hand column the number of children they were to have, the numbers in the corresponding row will tell us the number of possible outcomes.'

'Leaving heredity aside, of course.'

'Yes. This is a purely hypothetical notion. With two children, for example, there are three possibilities: two boys or one boy, and one girl or two girls. If you add up the numbers in that row, we have four. This tells us that the chances of having two boys are one in four, or having one child of each sex are two in four and of having two girls are again one in four.'

'I see.' Gautier looked at the triangle of numbers. 'So

135

in the case of four children, there is only one chance in sixteen of having all boys and six chances in sixteen of having two of each sex.'

'Precisely. And four chances in sixteen, or one in four, of having either one boy and three girls or the reverse. Now the triangle in this form is of no help to us with your problem, but I know a card trick based on it which may be. Let me show you.'

Taking the fifteen cards which Gautier had picked out, and also the remainder of the pack, the professor handed them to Gautier and told him to select five cards and place them in a row, face upwards on the desk. None of the cards he chose should be higher in value than a nine. Gautier shuffled through the pack, picked out five cards and laid them down.

Racine looked at the ones he had chosen for a moment, shuffled through the pack, took out another card and placed it face down on his desk some distance above the others. Then he told Gautier to construct a pyramid of cards by adding each pair of cards together and finding another one with a value equal to that sum to place above the pair. If the sum were to total more than nine, he should deduct nine from it and use a card equal to the remainder. Gautier did as he had been asked, and presently he had formed a row of four cards above the original five.

'Now do the same for those four cards,' Racine said.

'You can use cards of any suit. The choice of suit is immaterial.'

In a few moments the pyramid of cards was complete, with the card that the professor had chosen at the top, still face down.

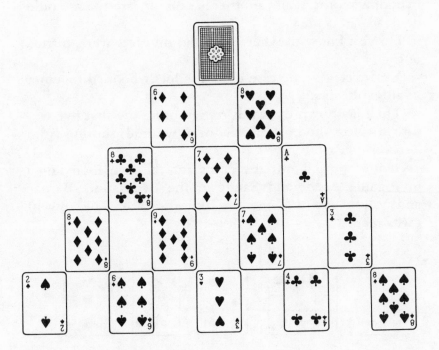

'As you can see,' the professor said, 'by adding the top pair of cards in your pyramid together we get the number fourteen, and if we subtract nine from that we have five.' Grinning, he turned the top card face upwards and showed that it was the five of hearts.

'With the help of Pascal's triangle, I was able to calculate what the top card in your pyramid must be as soon as you had laid out the bottom row. I won't tell you how.' He grinned again. 'You can work it out for yourself later. Let's call it your homework. But now we must consider your problem with the list of Condemned Ones. How many people did you say have been assassinated already by the madman behind this plot?'

'Five. And there have been unsuccessful attempts on the lives of two others, and another has disappeared so he could be dead.'

'Do you know in what order the murders were carried out?'

'Yes, except in the case of two sailors who died together in an explosion.'

'Then lay down the cards representing the first five victims to form the bottom row of a pyramid, starting from left to right.'

Gautier picked out the cards for the two men killed in Pigalle, Ardot and Sandeau, the two sailors Bernac and Villon and the one for Judge Lacaze. The row of cards read:

'The seven of diamonds and two of spades could be reversed,' Gautier remarked.

'We will soon find out. Give me all the other cards that appeared on the list of Condemned Ones.'

Taking the cards from Gautier, the professor constructed a pyramid.

'There! It works out perfectly,' Racine said. 'If you were to reverse the order of the seven of diamonds and the two of spades, the figures above them would be different

138

and the cards on your list would not fit into a pyramid pattern.'

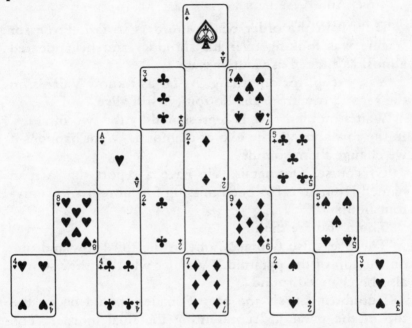

Gautier stared at the cards in disbelief. Listening to the professor, and as they were constructing the pyramid of cards, he had been too absorbed in the mental exercise to wonder whether it really might have any practical relationship to the murders he was investigating. It had been no more than a puzzle of numbers. Now his disbelief was replaced by a sudden excitement. The arrangement of the pyramid, fitting all the cards on the list of Condemned Ones, could not be mere coincidence. Taking a sheet of paper from the many that were littered about the professor's desk, he began translating the pyramid of cards into a pyramid of names.

Mounet

Fleury   Archard

Loubet   Desmarais   Grigov

Dubois   Valanis   Risson-Vernet   Rozière

Ardot   Sandeau   Bernac   Villon   Lacaze

'Does it fit the order of the murders so far?' Professor Racine was looking over his shoulder and he appeared almost as excited as Gautier was.

'Yes, except for one thing. As far as I know Valanis, in the second row from the bottom, is still alive.'

'Wait a moment. He is represented by the two of clubs. In the row above is the two of diamonds. What happens if we change them round?'

'Of course! Desmarais. We have a report that a man named Desmarais has been missing for more than twenty-four hours.'

'There you are then!'

'There are also two aces, one in the third row and one on the top of the pyramid. I wonder whether they should also be changed round.'

'I doubt it. Surely the ace of spades should be on the top of the pyramid, representing the final murder. The ace of spades is recognised as the symbol of death. Fifteen murders culminating in the ace of spades. What an elegant plot!'

Gautier folded the sheet of paper on which he had written the names and put it in his pocket. As he was gathering the playing cards together, he asked Racine, 'Who would know about Pascal's triangle?'

'Almost anyone who had studied mathematics to an advanced level.'

'Or physics?'

'Yes, they are closely related. Pascal was really a philosopher, so anyone reading his works might be interested enough to study his triangle as well.'

When Gautier left, the professor led him out on to the landing outside his study. Pointing to the four flights of stairs below them, he said, 'I must apologise for bringing you all the way up to this eyrie.'

'Not at all, Professeur, the climb proved to be well worth while.'

'In one way it is appropriate that a man as tall as I should work at the top of a building.' Racine smiled at Gautier in the manner of a man who has a joke he must tell. 'You would agree, Inspecteur, that I am not exactly a stupid man?'

'Of course not. Your career and many achievements prove that.'

'As a tall, gangling and clumsy boy I used to be self-conscious about my height. Now, one of my private satisfactions is that I have proved Bacon, the English philosopher, wrong.'

'In what way?'

'Bacon once remarked that in tall people, as in tall houses, the top floor is generally the least furnished.'

When he arrived back at the Sûreté, Gautier was still enjoying the amusement of his visit to the professor. In an age when it had become fashionable to cultivate bizarre affectations and manners likely to startle or shock, Racine was one of the few genuine eccentrics, and to be admired for that reason.

His amusement evaporated when he saw the message which was handed to him as he passed through the entrance of the Sûreté headquarters. Would Inspector Gautier go at once to Bagnolet, where the watchmaker Ribot had been found murdered.

12

Ribot had lived in an apartment above his small shop in a mean street not far from an abattoir. It may have been the constant presence of death in its most cruel and squalid form that created the atmosphere of hopeless gloom which seemed to hang over the *quartier*. The watchmaker's body, covered by a blanket, lay in the apartment waiting to be taken to the mortuary, for a doctor had already been, examined the body and left. Gautier lifted the blanket and saw that Ribot's throat had been cut, just as brutally and as finally as the throats of the beasts were cut in the nearby abattoir. The nightshirt he had been wearing had been soaked in blood and a pool of blood, rapidly drying, had formed on the linoleum beneath the body, which lay at the head of the stairs leading down to the shop. It had been found there that morning by the woman who came to clean and cook for Ribot, whose wife had died some years previously and who had been living alone.

'It looks as though he heard an intruder in the shop during the night,' Surat told Gautier, 'came out of the bedroom to see what was happening and was attacked here.'

'Possibly.'

'See! He had armed himself.' Surat pointed at the handle of an axe or hatchet which lay on the floor not far from the body.

'His murder has come at a very convenient time for whoever contrived the plan to place that bomb in the Palais de Justice. Now Ribot will answer no more questions.'

The two of them went downstairs and looked around the shop. It had a small workshop at the rear which was full of watchmaker's instruments and a large number of clocks and watches, some waiting to be repaired, others already repaired and being tested. Gautier was surprised by the cacophony of noise and contrasting rhythms produced by so many timepieces, each with its own beat, none of them synchronised. To make a person listen to them in such a confined space for any length of time might be an effective form of torture.

'One may assume that robbery was not the motive for the murder,' Gautier remarked. 'Nothing much can have been taken.'

Three policemen from the local commissariat had been in the premises when Gautier arrived and he put two of them to work searching the shop for any material that might have been used to make bombs. He did not expect that they would find anything, for Ribot had struck him as a clever, methodical man and he would have been alerted when he learnt that he had been recognised carrying his package into the law courts. Meanwhile he went upstairs with Surat to look round the apartment.

There were only three rooms, a reasonably spacious living room heated by an iron stove, a small bedroom and an even smaller kitchen. The tidy cleanliness of the place was more evidence of Ribot's methodical nature. Gautier began searching the living room, starting with the heavy sideboard in which not only the crockery and cutlery were kept, but also tins and bottles and packets of provisions, for there was no space for them in the kitchen.

'What are we looking for, patron?' Surat asked.

'Money. If he made that bomb he would have been well paid, and men with Ribot's record do not trust banks.'

They looked together in all the hiding places which, in their experience, people used when they had money to conceal, some unbelievably improbable, others more

143

cunningly chosen: in saucepans, beneath paper used to line drawers, in a mattress or the stuffing of cushions, buried in jars of coffee or sugar or cooking salt, in the lining of a coat, the backing of a cheap, framed print of the Eiffel Tower. Eventually Gautier found 165 francs hidden below the inner sole of one of a pair of boots in the bedroom. He held the notes up to Surat.

'This does not seem much of a reward for all the risks involved in making a bomb and taking it into the Palais de Justice.'

'Perhaps he had spent the rest.'

'On what? Debauchery and women? He scarcely had time for that. In any case, Ribot gave one the impression of being a cautious, thrifty man.'

'Do you think he was telling the truth and that he did not make the bomb?'

'Not for a moment. We'll keep on searching.'

They found no more money except for a few sous in a tin box in the kitchen. On a shelf above the sideboard stood half-a-dozen books and Gautier picked them up one by one, shaking them to see if any banknotes might be concealed between the pages. The fourth book he handled was a slim volume, bound in leather and with the title embossed on the spine in gold letters. When he opened it he realised that, apart from the binding, it was a very old book, for the pages were yellow with age and printed in a style of typeface totally unlike anything he had seen in contemporary books. As far as he could tell it was a treatise on astrology, for the text was illustrated with drawings of the planets and signs of the zodiac. He thought it a most unlikely book to find in the apartment of a craftsman of modest means.

When he left Bagnolet to return to the centre of Paris, he took the book with him. Before going he sealed Ribot's shop and apartment by fixing tape across the doors with official police seals and left one of the policemen on guard outside, the correct procedure in cases of murder. To earn Courtrand's approval for once might be a sensible precaution, for Gautier's intuition told him that the affair of the Condemned Ones was reaching a stage when he might feel impelled to follow his own, less orthodox methods.

To save time, as it was almost mid-day and he wished to reach the Café Corneille while the regular habitués were still there, he insisted on riding to the Ile de la Cité in a motor omnibus. Surat hated motor buses, partly because he had a superstitious distrust of the internal combustion engine and partly because of his concern for the future of the horse. When the motorised took over from the horse-drawn omnibuses, what would happen to the horses? he would ask. Automobiles were replacing private carriages and soon, no doubt, delivery vans and *fiacres* would give way to infernal engines. The Compagnie Générale, which owned most of the *fiacres* in Paris, had several thousand horses. What would be done with them? The English, Gautier was tempted to tell him, would say that the French would eat them, but he knew that Surat's concern for animals was genuine so he refrained from joking.

When their omnibus reached place de la Bastille, he climbed down, leaving Surat to continue to the Hôtel de Ville. From there he could walk to the Sûreté on Quai des Orfèvres and find out what Gautier wished to know. They agreed to meet and lunch together in the café in place Dauphine. Gautier meanwhile found a *fiacre* to take him along Boulevard St-Germain to the Café Corneille and was pleased when he saw that Duthrey, Froissart and the deputy for Val-de-Marne were all still there. After he had joined them and ordered himself a coffee and a kir, he showed the book he had found in Ribot's apartment to Froissart.

'What can you tell me about this?' he asked him.

Froissart took the book, examined its binding and then opened and studied the title-page minutely. Finally

145

he flicked though the other pages, turning them carefully as though afraid he might damage them.

'This is a very rare book,' he said, 'one that any collector would find interesting and which many would be glad to own. As you can see it was printed early in the seventeenth century and was written by Augustus Murch, a famous astrologer from Saxony. Is it yours?'

'No. You might say I have borrowed it.'

'Then take good care of it.' Froissart was too tactful to ask why, since Gautier had never shown any interest in astrology, he should have borrowed the book.

'Why, is it valuable?'

'Certainly. If it were offered for sale I would say it should fetch at least three thousand francs. A pity it has been rebound, though. The same book in its original binding might fetch double that sum.'

'Are you using your new-found wealth to start a book collection?' Duthrey asked Gautier slyly.

'What wealth?' the deputy asked.

'My colleague Vettard tells me that Gautier landed a big betting coup at Longchamp yesterday.'

'Some coup! I won four hundred and fifty francs.'

'Vettard is jealous because he bet on a different horse. He suspects that you must have had – what do they call it? – inside information.'

'How did you come to choose the winner?' Froissart asked.

'I would be too ashamed to tell you.'

They began discussing gambling, betting on horses at first and then gambling generally, the growing popularity of casinos at resorts and the moral issues involved. Duthrey viewed the spread of gambling as another symptom of the moral decline of the French people. He saw evidence of this too in the rapid increase in divorce, homosexuality, the taking of drugs and the formation of trade unions. Like many people he believed that the nation must be regenerated, spiritually as well as physically, to prepare itself for revenge on Germany. But not everyone shared his views and the debate at the Café Corneille that day became unusually animated without ever degenerating into acrimony.

When Gautier left the café, Duthrey walked a little way along Boulevard St-Germain with him. Gautier sensed that he had something he wished to say but preferred not to in front of their other friends.

'When you get back to the Sûreté,' he said finally, 'you may expect to find two journalists from *Figaro* there. Unless of course they have been pestering you already.'

'What do they want?'

'To know what is being done about the wave of crime that is sweeping through Paris. We have had two bombs, one in a boat and one in the law courts, and yesterday somebody tried to assassinate the Minister of Finance. Have the anarchists returned? *Figaro* wants to know the answer.'

'Frankly, we do not have it.'

'I'm only warning you, old friend. Crime, fortunately, is not a subject with which I have to concern myself.'

'Thank you for the warning.'

What Duthrey had told him only strengthened the resolution Gautier had already made to find reasons for not returning to Sûreté headquarters that afternoon. Other plans were forming in his mind and he had no wish to be given instructions which might prevent him from carrying them out. When he reached place Dauphine, Surat was already waiting for him in the café. They ordered their meal and ate without mentioning the affair of the Condemned Ones or any other police matters. Eating was not a mere biological function but a pleasure, and even a meal in a humble café should provide enjoyment and appreciation. Talking about work or worrying about it only spoilt the pleasure and could also give one indigestion. So Gautier and Surat chatted about his wife and family, interrupting

147

their conversation from time to time with comments on the *rognons de veau* and the *terrine* and the *tarte aux pommes*.

When they had finished eating, Gautier ordered a second carafe of wine and pulled out from his pocket the pack of cards and the sheet of paper which he had brought back from his visit to Professor Racine and on which he had written the names of the Condemned Ones in a pyramid. Briefly, he explained to Surat how the pyramid of cards was constructed and how it seemed to forecast the order in which the people of the list were being attacked, without mentioning the theory behind the calculations or Pascal's triangle.

'But why should anyone go to the trouble of inventing a plan like this?' Surat protested. 'Why not just kill the people on the list and have done with it?'

'Who knows? We will learn the answer to that eventually, no doubt, but in the meantime, if we are right about the plan, our work is made easier.'

'Because we know who the next victim is to be and can protect him?'

'Exactly.'

Surat looked at the pyramid of names. 'Then the next one to be attacked should be the deputy for Seine-Maritime, Claude Rozière.'

'Not necessarily. Look at the pyramid of cards. The next card is a five, but there are two fives on the list and we cannot be sure which of the two is intended to be next. It could be Rozière or the other five, Grigov the opera singer.'

That evening Gautier went to the opera. It was the first time he had visited the imposing opera house which stood at the head of Avenue de l'Opéra, since the evening when he had managed to frustrate an attempt to assassinate King Edward VII, who had been in Paris incognito and was attending a performance of *Tristan et Isolde*, accompanied in his box by one of his former mistresses. Returning to the scene of that dramatic evening did not evoke any memories of the incident itself or of the events leading up to it. That was a good sign, he decided, proving that he was not yet an old man finding enjoyment only in nostalgia.

He had gone to l'Opéra because Ivan Grigov was appearing that night in *Faust*. Earlier in the afternoon he had gone to the Hôtel Meurice where, Surat had established, Grigov was staying while he was in Paris. The Russian singer had received the two of them in his luxurious suite which overlooked rue de Rivoli and the Jardins des Tuileries. He was a stout man, but, in spite of his clumsy body, vain, for he was wearing what Gautier decided must be a toupée and had coloured his cheeks with rouge.

He had asked them if they had any news, for he had already been warned that his name was on the list of Condemned Ones. 'One more person on the list has been attacked,' Gautier had replied, 'and one has disappeared.'

'So it appears we must take these threats seriously.'

'Without doubt. And we have reason to believe that you may be the next intended victim.'

'Are you certain of that?'

'No, Monsieur. In our opinion it will either be you or one other gentleman.'

'What do you want me to do?'

'The wisest course would be for you to stay in your suite here in the hotel, at least for the next day or two. The management will no doubt send your meals up and we will station policemen on guard in the corridor outside and elsewhere in the hotel.'

'That is totally impossible. I have a performance to-night.'

Gautier and Surat had tried to argue with him that he should cancel his appearance in *Faust* that evening and allow his understudy to sing the part, but Grigov would not be persuaded. The role of Mephistopheles was too important to be sung by an understudy, and in any event

149

people had bought tickets for the performance expecting to see and hear him.

'I do not renege on my commitments lightly,' he had said, and then, looking at Gautier sternly, he had added, 'although people may have led you to believe that I do.'

In the end, all he had agreed to, reluctantly, was that he would remain in the Meurice until it was time for him to leave for the performance and that two policemen should escort him to the opera house and back to his hotel afterwards. He would give no undertaking beyond that.

After leaving him, Gautier and Surat had gone to call on Claude Rozière who lived with his wife in an apartment in Avenue de Suffren on the Left Bank. Rozière had been easier to convince that precautions should be taken to protect his life and one had the impression that he was not a courageous man, although he put on a façade of manliness. He had told Gautier that he had intended in any case to leave Paris the next day to spend a few days in a house which he owned in the country, not far from Rouen. On Gautier's advice he had agreed to change his plans. He would go to the railway station with his wife, board a train as though intending to travel to his country home, leave the train at the first convenient stop and find an inn in the country where he could stay incognito for a few days.

'Read the newspapers every day,' Gautier had advised him, 'and you will be able to judge when it is safe for you to return to Paris.'

Rozière and his wife had packed their valises and left almost immediately in a *fiacre* for the railway station. Gautier and Surat had followed them at a distance in another *fiacre* and waited at the station until they had boarded a train. So far as they had been able to see no one had been watching the deputy and his wife and no one had followed them on to the train. Surat had then gone off duty, reluctantly, Gautier insisting that he should spend what was left of the day with his family. Gautier himself had gone to his apartment and changed into evening clothes, for he wished to be inconspicuous among the audience at the opera.

He had arrived at the opera house more than an hour before the performance of *Faust* was due to begin, which had given him time to refresh his memory of the geography of the place. As he toured the rooms where the performers changed, the *foyer de danse* where gentlemen subscribers were allowed to meet and pay court to the ladies of the ballet, the front and main foyers, the long buffet gallery and the vast staircases which led to the upper floors, he tried to imagine where an assassin would be most likely to attack a singer and what method he would use. A bomb could probably be ruled out since, on the instructions of the Prefect of Police, l'Opéra and all other public buildings were being regularly searched for bombs. Similarly an attack with a knife, like the one at Longchamp, was unlikely, for the assassin would not be allowed entry either to the changing rooms or behind the stage. That meant in all probability using a pistol or revolver to shoot Grigov while he was on stage.

The auditorium of the opera house was horseshoe-shaped, richly decorated in red and gold and with an ornate ceiling symbolising the hours of day and night, from which hung a vast gas chandelier. Facing the stage were rows of seats and behind them three tiers of boxes right around the auditorium with a tier of *baignoires* below and a gallery above. To shoot at a performer on the stage from one of the seats near the front of the auditorium would be relatively simple, but, surrounded by the rest of the audience and with attendants stationed at all exits, the person firing the shot would have virtually no chance of escaping. That left the boxes. The boxes at each end of the three tiers overlooked the stage, and at times during the performance a singer might be only a few metres from them. The box in the lowest tier would give the shortest range, but the boxes in the tiers above, and indeed any box one along from the end of a tier, would be close enough for a shot to have a reasonable chance of hitting its target. It was from one of these twelve boxes, six on each side of the stage, Gautier decided, that any attempt to shoot Ivan Grigov would be made.

He wished now that he had brought Surat and more policemen with him. The best way of preventing any attack on Grigov would have been to keep a watch on everyone who entered all of the twelve boxes, which would have meant stationing a man at each end of each tier to watch the entrances to the last pair of boxes, six policemen in all. Now it was too late to send for reinforcements, as early arrivals among the audience for the performance were already coming in to the opera house and making their way up the staircases to the upper floors. Attendants were standing in the corridor that ran round the back of each tier of boxes, waiting to open them to the people in whose names they had been reserved.

Gautier went up to one of the attendants and explained who he was. 'Would there be a list of people who have reserved boxes for tonight's performance?'

'The management will have a list, yes, Monsieur.'

'Where would I be able to see it?'

'Downstairs in the office, but it will not tell you what you wish to know.'

'Why should that be?'

'Many of the boxes are reserved for regular subscribers and very often these people will not use their boxes, but put them at the disposal of friends. It has even been known for subscribers to sell the use of their boxes for a performance to visitors from overseas,' the attendant added, in a tone which showed his disapproval of those who abused their privilege in this way.

'Will all the boxes be occupied tonight, do you suppose?'

'I doubt it, Monsieur. Monday is opera night for *le monde* and the bourgeoisie prefer more robust pleasures on Saturday nights; the *caf'conc'*, the dance halls, the Moulin Rouge.'

The man promised that once the performance started he would make enquiries among the other attendants to see whether there was an empty box which the inspector could use. There was nothing more Gautier could do then but watch the audience as they arrived and made their way to their seats or boxes. Many of them stopped to talk with friends whom they recognised in the main foyer at the head of the staircase from the front foyer or in the two rotundas which led off it. He saw no one whom he might suspect of wanting to murder Grigov, but in the 1,500 or so people who were crowding into the building it was not likely that he would glimpse a face he recognised.

Shortly after he heard the first chords of the overture, the attendant to whom he had spoken came and led him to a vacant box. There were thirty-nine boxes in each tier and he had been given one in the top tier not too far from the stage. It offered a good vantage point from which he could look into a very large proportion of the boxes around the auditorium opposite him, and, if he leant forward, into the boxes nearest to the stage on the same side as his own.

The scene on the stage was Faust's study as dawn was breaking. The aged philosopher, depressed by the futility of a life wasted in trying vainly to solve the riddle of the universe and jealous of the youth of the young men and women who were singing outside his window on their way to work, cursed his advancing age and called on Satan to help him. There was a flash of red light, out of which, rising up through the stage, came Mephistopheles.

From his apartment Gautier had brought with him a powerful pair of binoculars and, ignoring the drama on the stage, he used them to look into every box within his view, sweeping the curve of the horseshoe slowly. Each box

153

could hold six people, except the presidential box and the boxes above it, which could seat ten. The President's box was not occupied that evening and many of the others were not full. It was not until he had looked into every box in the upper tier and was half-way along the middle row that he saw anyone he knew.

Paul Valanis was seated next to an extremely pretty girl who could not have been much more than nineteen or twenty and who, Gautier guessed, must be his latest mistress, the Antoinette after whom his houseboat had been renamed. They were accompanied by four people, two couples rather younger than Valanis but a good deal older than the girl, invited no doubt to chaperone her.

Continuing his scrutiny, Gautier swept the lowest tier and saw that in the box immediately next to the one overlooking the stage there was a woman sitting on her own. He supposed he should have been surprised when he recognised her as Princesse Sophia Dashkova, but he was not.

For several minutes he watched her through the binoculars. She was wearing evening dress, as almost all the ladies in the boxes were, a crimson dress too bright, one would have thought, if she wished to remain inconspicuous, and she sat motionless watching the opera, but not intently, for the expression on her face was one of distant melancholy. On the stage, Grigov singing the role of Mephistopheles was sharing a duet with Faust who, having signed his soul away, had regained his youth and gallantry.

In a few moments the first act would come to an end, and Gautier realised what he must do. Leaving his box, he hurried down two floors by the staircase and around the back of the lowest tier of boxes to the one in which the princess was sitting. The door to the box was locked, but this was not unusual for the management recognised that its clients, especially gentlemen who might be accompanied by their mistresses, expected privacy once they were in their boxes.

Gautier knocked on the door and waited. Then, conscious that the music from the stage might drown a single rap, he knocked again more loudly.

Presently the princess opened the door. 'Monsieur Gautier!' She appeared more confused than surprised.

'May I come in?'

Her hesitation was only momentary. 'Of course.' When he was inside and she had shut the door she asked him, 'What are you doing here?'

'I was up there in a box opposite you, saw you were alone and decided to ask whether I might join you.'

'That would give me great pleasure.' She did not appear to have noticed that he had not answered her question.

They sat down, but almost immediately the curtain came down at the end of the first act. A performance at l'Opéra was a long and leisurely business, with intervals between each of the acts, allowing audiences to stretch their legs and relax in the foyers and on the balconies or go to the long buffet gallery.

'May I offer you some refreshment?' Gautier asked.

'That would be very pleasant but the buffet becomes so crowded.'

'Leave matters to me.'

Opening the door of the box, Gautier beckoned to an attendant who was standing not far away. Giving him money, he asked him to arrange for a waiter to bring a bottle of champagne to the princess's box.

When he went back to her, the princess said, 'I suppose you are wondering why I am here alone. The truth is that I had invited two guests to share this box, but one of them was taken ill.'

'How very unfortunate!'

'They are two very old and dear friends of mine – Russians who have come to live in voluntary exile in France.'

The princess paused, looked at Gautier for a moment and then continued to tell him about her friends. They were a grand duke and his wife, close friends of the parents of her husband the prince, who had given her great comfort and support after his death. Troubled by the growing political unrest in Russia and afraid of what might happen to the aristocracy were there to be a revolution, they had decided to emigrate, selling their property and coming to live in Paris.

'They were to come with me tonight,' the princess concluded, 'but the duchess was suddenly taken ill.'

'That must have been disappointing for them.'

'And for me. The duke would not leave the duchess on her own. They are both very old and nervous. One can understand what it must be like for old people who have just arrived to live in a foreign country.'

Princesse Sophia appeared to feel she was obliged to explain her appearance alone at the opera that evening at length, giving corroborative details in case her story might not be believed. A waiter arriving with a bottle of Mumm champagne gave Gautier the opportunity to steer their conversation away from a subject which seemed to make her uncomfortable.

'Mumm Cordon Rouge,' he said, holding up the champagne bottle. 'They say it was the favourite champagne of Edward when he was Prince of Wales and that as well as drinking it he used to fill a silver bath with it for his favourite mistress.'

'What a waste of champagne!'

'I agree.'

While they were drinking, Gautier took his binoculars and focused them on the box in which he had seen Paul Valanis. He saw that the Greek and his guests were also drinking champagne. The pretty girl seemed excited and happy, and one could tell from the way in which she looked at Valanis and laid her hand on his arm that she was strongly attracted to him.

'Your eyesight must be very poor,' Princesse Sophia remarked.

'Why do you say that?' Gautier replied without taking the binoculars from his eyes.

'Most people can manage with opera glasses.'

'Ah, but I am a good deal more inquisitive than most people!'

'I don't believe you are here to watch the opera at all. You are keeping watch on someone.'

'A policeman's work never ends!'

'Who is it you're spying on?'

Instead of replying, Gautier handed her the binoculars and the princess trained them on the box which he had been watching. 'I was wrong!' she exclaimed. 'You are just mesmerised by that very lovely girl! Voyeur! Who is she?'

'Unless I am mistaken, she is the granddaughter of Admiral Pottier.'

'And the man beside him?'

'Paul Valanis.'

The expression on the princess's face hardened and Gautier noticed her knuckles turn white as her grip on the binoculars tightened, but she made no comment. Instead, after a few seconds, she swung the binoculars slowly away from Valanis and his party and looked down on the rows of seats in the auditorium beneath them, which were filling up as people returned from the interval. She did not lower the glasses until the curtain was rising for the second act, and then she handed them to Gautier.

They watched the second act in silence, but by the time the next interval came she had regained her composure and they talked about the opera, the performances of the leading singers, the music and the stage sets. The princess appeared particularly interested in the ballet. Up to that time, she told him, ballet had been no more than an append-age to opera, stifled in a straitjacket of classical tradition with the same costumes, the same gracefully pretty steps, an innocent but meaningless diversion. But now in Russia a new ballet was being born, with daring innovations in choreography, exciting, passionate music and dazzling sets. Before long, she was certain, a Russian ballet company would come to Paris and create a sensation.

In the next interval they started on a second bottle of champagne. As he was filling her glass, the princess remarked, 'I am glad you saw me with your spy glasses and came to join me, or my evening would have been ruined.'

'I am glad too.'

'The illness of the duchess is going to spoil my day tomorrow as well.'

'Why is that?'

'I was planning to spend the day showing the two of them something of Paris.'

'Could I take their place?' Gautier made the suggestion on an impulse, but it was not through gallantry. A plan was forming in his mind.

'Do you think I could show you Paris?' she asked, laughing at him.

'Probably not. But I could take you somewhere outside the city which I am sure you would enjoy.'

'I accept with pleasure.'

'Then I'll meet you at the Gare St-Lazare at noon. Don't wear anything too smart.'

'It sounds like an adventure.'

'It may well be.'

13

As he lay back in the barber's chair, enjoying the luxury of being shaved, Gautier was thinking not of the afternoon to come, but of what he had done that morning. The barber, an enterprising man who was willing to work on Sunday mornings, had his shop very near the Gare St-Lazare and Gautier would have only to cross the street into the station forecourt when the time came for him to meet Princesse Sophia. Before going to the barber's he had called at the Sûreté and, after some difficulty, found a clerk to open the records section, in which special files were kept on all foreigners entering France who had criminal records in their own country or were thought likely to cause trouble for the police in the future.

Gautier knew that there was a dossier on Paul Valanis among the records, for he had found one when he first came across the man during his investigations of the murder of the Montmartre art dealer. He recalled the various offences which Valanis had committed in Turkey and Greece – smuggling, fraudulent deals and handling stolen property – and the ways in which he had managed to talk himself out of trouble. What he could not remember were the dates when the offences had been committed. When he had looked through the dossier again that morning, he had found that Valanis was fifty-one, older than he had expected, and that he had left Turkey to escape prison when he was thirty-two. Most of his criminal activities seemed to have taken place in the five years preceding that.

While he was being shaved, Gautier thought over the implications of what he had found out and also about the events of the last twenty-four hours. Claude Rozière was hidden safely outside Paris and Grigov had agreed to stay in his hotel under police guard for the whole of Sunday. These precautions may have bought time, but nothing more. Gautier tried to imagine what the person who had planned the murders of the Condemned Ones would do next. Was he determined to attack his victims in the order dictated by the pyramid of cards? Would he be prepared to wait until an opportunity to strike at Rozière or Grigov arrived. They could not be protected for ever. Or would he pass on to his next victim? A five, either the five of clubs or the five of spades, had been the last in the row of four cards. If the assassin kept to his plan, the next victim would be represented by the first card in the row of three cards above, and this was an ace. There were two aces in the list, the ace of hearts against the name of Emile Loubet, the President of the Republic, and the ace of spades against Jacques Mounet.

The logical course would be for the Sûreté to take protective measures for Loubet and Mounet similar to those Gautier had taken for Rozière and Grigov. But that again would only be buying time, postponing the assassination attempts. The only ultimate solution to the problem was to discover who was the author of the plan and responsible for the murders so far committed. The barber had finished his work and put down his razor. As he lay back in the chair, enjoying the soothing balm of hot towels on his face and neck, Gautier thought gloomily that perhaps the progress which he had begun to believe he was making was illusory, and that the affair of the Condemned Ones, like many of the other criminal cases in which he had been involved, might be resolved only when it was too late to save lives.

As he left the barber's shop and walked across the street to the Gare St-Lazare, he put pessimism behind him, telling

160

himself that every day he moved a little nearer to learning the truth. Intuition told him, too, that this Sunday would be no exception, and he would learn a little more. He had scarcely taken up a position at the entrance to the station, with almost ten minutes to go before the time for their rendez-vous, when a *fiacre* pulled up in front of him and Princesse Sophia climbed down to meet him.

'Have I disgraced myself?' she asked him.

'What makes you think that?'

'Ladies are not supposed to be early for a rendez-vous with a gentleman. That's what the Americans call being fast.'

'But surely we arranged to meet at eleven-thirty?'

'What a gallant lie! Now I feel much better.'

As they went into the station, making for the platform from which trains on the St-Germain line would leave, she asked him. 'How do I look?'

'Perfect.'

'Dowdy and inconspicuous as you asked?'

'You could never look dowdy.'

'And you!' She pointed to the straw boater Gautier was wearing. 'How dashing!'

'A *canotier* is *de rigueur* on the river.'

'Does that mean we are going boating?'

'Who knows? We are going to a *guinguette* by the Seine where anything might happen.'

'Wonderful!' The princess clapped her hands. 'I've heard so much about them. Will there be dancing?'

'Yes, and eating and drinking. A really bacchanalian afternoon.'

The *ginguettes* in the outer *quartiers* of Paris were where working people went to enjoy themselves. At all of them one could eat, drink and dance, and some had booths and shooting galleries and roundabouts, so that they were really small pleasure gardens. For those who liked their recreations strenuous, noisy and uninhibited, *guinguettes* offered an invigorating way of spending a Sunday afternoon.

Gautier had decided to take the princess to one of the *guinguettes* at Asnières, a village on the Seine only a few minutes by train from Paris on the Ligne de St-Germain. He knew that as well as a number of *guinguettes*, Asnières had a modest but comfortable hotel, where he had lunched more than once with his wife and her parents when she was alive and to which he could take Princesse Sophia if the pleasures of ordinary people proved too robust for her.

He need not have worried. The *guinguette* they chose was called Le Gallant Jardinier, and it was plain from the start that Princesse Sophia was delighted with its ambience of noisy good humour. The food, mainly roast meats cooked on spits, was prepared on a range in the gardens large enough and hot enough to look like a huge forge, the wine was strong and stout in body, the music lively enough to persuade even the most reluctant to dance. The manners of the customers were a good deal less rough than in the *guinguettes* of Belleville and Ménilmontant. There, if a man wished to dance with a girl, he would approach her directly and even snatch her from her partner if he was confident he could win the inevitable fight that followed. At the table next to Sophia and Gautier there was a party of six, an employee of the railways, one from the Compagnie de Gaz and another from the department store La Samaritaine, two with their wives and the third with his fiancée. Before long Sophia and Gautier were laughing and joking with them.

'Christian names only, mind,' Sophia whispered to Gautier. 'Either of our titles would be an embarrassment to them.'

And so Sophia and Jean-Paul spent the afternoon with Arlette and Luc, Berthe and Pierre, Marie-France and Jean. Watching the princess, Gautier was astonished at her appetite, not only for the simple food and ordinary wine they shared with the others, but for gaiety. She danced with every man in the group, not conscious, it seemed, of the bizarre contrast which there must be between the vigorous, unrestrained dances of a *guinguette* and the measured waltzes which she must have danced at the Russian imperial court.

They were all drinking freely, and late in the afternoon Luc, the young shop assistant from La Samaritaine, began to show signs that too much alcohol made him aggressive as well as lecherous. Gautier noticed that when the princess was dancing with him she was kept busy restraining his groping hands. Before long a scene would be inevitable, jealousy on the part of Luc's wife, angry remarks, faces slapped and perhaps even a fight. Gautier had seen it all before.

'Would you care to go on the river before it is too late?' he asked Sophia.

'Would you?'

'That's why I brought my *canotier*, remember.'

The two of them left the others at the *guinguette* amicably, with promises that they would all meet again soon, perhaps the next Sunday, perhaps the one after, and made their way to the Hôtel de Paris which stood overlooking the Seine, and outside which there was a landing stage from which one could hire rowing boats. A river ran through the village in the country where Gautier had been born and he had learnt to handle a boat and to swim and to fish while he was very young. Although he had seldom been on the water since he came to Paris, the skill had not left him. He helped Sophia into the boat which they hired and made her sit opposite him in the stern, while he took the oars. She took off the hat she was wearing and let her fingers trail in the water as he pulled them away from the river bank.

'Are you sure you are all right? The sun is hotter than I thought it would be.'

'I'm fine; loving it!'

'Perhaps we should have brought a parasol for you.'

'Don't be absurd!' She laughed. 'Can you imagine what I would look like sitting here with a parasol?'

Out in the river he swung the boat round until it was pointing upstream, and soon they had left Asnières behind them. Looking back, Gautier saw that it was still no more than a village, but Paris, he knew, was spreading and soon no doubt Asnières would be swallowed up by the city just as villages like Montmartre, Belleville and Ménilmontant had been. To see them lose their character and their independence made him sad.

'The other evening,' he told Sophia, 'when I saw that miniature portrait of your cousin, I had the feeling that I had seen her somewhere before.'

'That's impossible. She was never in France.'

'Jacques Mounet has a portrait of a girl exactly like her in his apartment.' Again Gautier saw a crushing melancholy in Sophia's face, but he knew he must ask another question. 'Your cousin was the girl who became Mounet's mistress in Turkey, wasn't she?'

'Yes.' Her reply was barely audible, her eyes full of unshed tears.

'Is that why you hate him?' Gautier hoped his question would convey the sympathy he felt.

'No.' Sophia blinked as though that would dispel her tears. 'To blame a man for seducing a woman is wrong. The woman who allows herself to become involved in an affair always knows what she is doing, however young she may be. In the case of my cousin, she grabbed the happiness that Mounet offered her. She was the fourth, the youngest and easily the loveliest of her husband's wives. The other wives and his concubines were jealous of her and expressed their jealousy in bullying and taunts. No, I don't blame Mounet for the affair nor its outcome. What I cannot forgive is the way he exploited it in that despicable novel, degrading both my cousin and their love for his own ends.'

They rowed on in silence. Another question was poised

ready in Gautier's mind, but he did not have the heart to ask it then. The sun was beginning to set and its slanting rays, reflected from the ripples which the breeze made on the water, were losing their hard brightness. Evening would come swiftly, so he turned the boat round in a wide arc and began making for Asnières. As they drew nearer to the village, they could hear music and laughter from other *guinguettes* along the river banks, Le Boeuf-Rouge, Le Coq-Hardi and Chez Papa Didi.

Sophia shivered. 'It's turning cold.'

'Take my jacket and put it round your shoulders.' Before starting to row, Gautier had taken off his coat and laid it on the bottom of the boat.

'What about you?'

'I shall not get cold as long as I keep rowing.'

'Is it strenuous?'

'Not too strenuous. Would you like to try?'

'May I? I would love to!' The last traces of Sophia's melancholy disappeared in excitement. Gautier admired her resilience.

'We'll have to change places.'

They managed the manoeuvre, but only with difficulty. Gautier had to hold Sophia's hands as she moved unsteadily towards him and to check the rocking of the boat at the same time. When he had her seated safely next to him he moved back to the stern. The first strokes which she attempted with the oars were a fiasco. She plunged the blade of one so deep into the water that she could not move it, while the other flapped ineffectively over the surface, throwing a spray up all over Gautier's legs.

'This was a mistake!' she called out laughing.

'Keep trying. Use short, shallow strokes.'

Her attempts to do what he told her made them both laugh. The boat swung first one way and then the other as she heaved on the oars with a complete lack of coordination. They were less than a hundred metres from the landing stage outside the hotel but they were making no progress and, if anything, were drifting further away from it.

'I give up,' Sophia said. 'Unless we plan to spend the night on the river, you had better take command of this vessel again.'

Leaving the oars trailing in the water, she got to her feet and, without waiting for Gautier to help her, walked towards him. After only two steps she lost her balance, and as she lurched one way the boat tilted sharply. Gautier reached out to grab her but she swayed backwards and away from him, losing control and stumbling. For a moment it seemed as though she had regained her balance, then she staggered back as the boat rocked from side to side. Briefly she stood poised unsteadily, her arms whirling in circles like a drunken tightrope walker. Then, with one final lurch, she toppled over the side into the water.

She did not sink immediately, kept afloat by the threshing of her arms and the buoyancy of air trapped in her skirts. Gautier realised at once that she could not swim and, grabbing one of the oars, thrust it towards her, shouting at her to seize it. She did, and as soon as he saw that her momentary panic had passed, he pulled her with the oar into the side of the boat.

Getting her into the boat was more difficult, for when he leant over the side and tried to pull her out of the water, it tilted steeply and threatened to capsize. People in other boats nearby had seen what had happened and one of them, a skilled oarsman, came to their help. He drew his boat alongside theirs on the opposite side to where Sophia was and, by pressing down on it, held it steady while Gautier, struggling against the weight of her sodden clothes, pulled her out of the river. She sat in the boat, shivering but laughing, as he rowed them to the landing stage with a few swift strokes.

166

'What do we do now?' she asked, clambering out of the boat.

'You could change your clothes in the hotel.' He pointed towards the Hôtel de Paris. 'Can you manage to walk there or shall I look for a *fiacre*?'

'Of course I can. Even a duck could waddle that far.'

She took his arm as they walked to the hotel. People whom they passed, seeing that no harm had come to her, laughed at them and Sophia laughed back, exchanging good-humoured banter with them.

'Eh, *chérie*, did the dirty pig try to drown you?'

'Not at all. He's a fisherman and when he saw I was too small he threw me back in the water.'

The management of the Hôtel de Paris could not have been more accommodating, putting a room at the princess's disposal. A tin bath was taken to the room and chambermaids began hurrying up and down the stairs, filling it with jugs of hot water from the kitchen. When the princess had taken off her wet clothes, they were taken away to be washed and ironed and a search started for something she could wear while this was being done. Gautier's coat and waistcoat, which were damp and creased, were also taken away to be pressed and he sat in the hotel's restaurant drinking brandy while he waited for them.

After twenty minutes or so, when he calculated that she would have finished her bath, he took the bottle of brandy, a jug of hot water and a glass upstairs. After knocking on the door of the room she had been given, he opened it a few inches and called out, 'I've brought you brandy and hot water to drink so that you won't catch cold. I'll leave it here outside in the corridor.'

'No, come on in,' Sophia called back. 'I've finished bathing and could use your help.'

Gautier went in and found her, wrapped in only a towel, sitting in front of the dressing table. She was drying her hair with another towel and held it out to him.

167

'Long hair like mine is impossible to dry without help.'

As he took the towel he remembered occasions when his wife too had asked him to dry her hair. The memory, unlike many that had come to him soon after Suzanne had died, did not bring feelings of guilt, only nostalgia. Suzanne often complained, affectionately, that he was too rough, so now he dried Sophia's hair gently and carefully. He noticed that her shoulders were fine-boned, more slender than Suzanne's, who had inclined to plumpness, and, looking at her, was conscious of her nakedness beneath the towel. Glancing up at the mirror on the dressing table, he saw that she was watching him.

'Wait,' she said suddenly, 'the towel is slipping.'

To refasten the towel around her she had to stand up, and as she opened it briefly he saw the length of her back, her slim waist, her haunches. Desire clutched at him and when, unable to restrain himself, he put his hands on her shoulders, she turned round, stared at him solemnly and then held up her face to him.

He kissed her and she gave her mouth to him freely, her arms encircling his neck. They kissed passionately but without haste, like lovers who had learnt how to arouse each other and who need not concern themselves with the urgency of time's winged chariot. And the kiss ended only when they heard a knock on the door.

'That will be the chambermaid, bringing me clothes to wear.'

'I'll wait for you downstairs.'

As he waited in the restaurant, a recurring picture of Sophia's nakedness came to him, flickering before his mind like the images of the cinematograph machine invented by the brothers Lumière, which he had once seen demonstrated in Paris. When she came down to join him she was wearing a black dress, stiff and formal in cut, which did not fit her and which looked as though it might be one of the dresses which the wife of the hotel proprietor

168

might wear when she was working. If Gautier had told the woman that Sophia was a princess, no doubt a silk dress would have been produced for her to wear. What bourgeois woman could have resisted the thought of being able to tell her friends that her best dress had once been borrowed by a Russian princess?

'Shall we dine while we are here?' Gautier asked. 'The food is not bad as I recall and by the time we finish eating they should have your clothes washed and pressed.'

'What a good idea! Let's eat now. I'm famished!'

'You can't be hungry already after the lunch we had!'

'I am. It must be all that rowing.'

As they dined in the restaurant, which overlooked the Seine, she talked about the afternoon, saying how much she had enjoyed it. Gautier was amused by what many would see as her almost childish excitement. He had seen different facets of her character at Madame Mauberge's salon and at the Pavillon d'Armenonville. She was sophisticated and cultured, able to win the admiration of people in society and to talk intelligently with playwrights and actors, but still had retained a captivating innocence.

'You told me that your father had been cheated out of all his money.'

'Yes, and he lost his business as well.'

'Was Paul Valanis the swindler?'

Sophia appeared astonished. 'Heavens no! As far as I know my father never even met Valanis. I was too young at the time to remember the details but I was told later that it was an Egyptian who defrauded my father; an Arab named Abdul Khalir.'

'You seem to dislike Valanis and I thought that might be the reason.'

'I don't know the man so I can't dislike him, but I disapprove of his behaviour. Like Jacques Mounet he has hurt my country. Yes, I know he's Greek, but people associate him with Turkey and they judge the Turks by

169

his behaviour. Our reputation is bad enough without our having to suffer for his misdeeds.'

Gautier could understand the reasons for her complaint. Turkey was regarded with odium by the rest of Europe, in some ways unfairly. People who had never been to Turkey and knew nothing of its history and culture condemned the Turks as barbarians, measuring a country that had never embraced Christianity by Christian ethics. At the same time he could not help feeling that Sophia was being excessively sensitive on the subject.

Their dinner was long and leisurely, as though by un-spoken consent they wished it to last as long as it could. By the time they finished the night was quiet, the sound of laughter and music faded, the *guinguettes* empty, Parisians on their way back into the city for the early Monday morning that would follow. Gautier remembered how as a boy he would open his bedroom window and look out on the fields, smell the scent of hay and wildflowers, hear the distant cry of a night bird and wish that the peace of the moment could be prolonged for ever. But presently the proprietor of the hotel, attentive and courteous, was at his elbow.

'Monsieur, Madame, did you enjoy your dinner?'

'Very much, thank you.'

'Will you be spending the night with us? It is late to be returning to Paris and Madame's clothes are not quite ready.'

Gautier hesitated. Suddenly he could not look at Sophia. Then he heard her say, firmly, 'We will, Monsieur, thank you.'

After the proprietor had left them she reached out and placed her hand on Gautier's, smiled at him, but said nothing. Soon afterwards they went upstairs and she undressed, modestly but without any show of coy-ness, and when he lay naked beside her she turned out the lamp which stood beside the bed. She was smaller than Gautier had imagined, with slim hips and thighs and tiny breasts.

When he touched her breasts, she asked, 'Do they please you?'

'Of course.'

'They are not too small?'

'They're exquisite.'

His answer was not insincere. He had always been attracted by women with full breasts and had come to assume that they were essential to voluptuousness, but Sophia's seemed to offer an almost virginal innocence, which both moved and excited him. After they had made love she lay for a time with her head on his shoulder. Then she got out of bed, crossed the room to the windows and drew the curtains. A moon had risen, and as she stood looking out across the river her body was silhouetted against its light.

When she climbed back into bed beside him, she asked, 'When we went back to my house after dinner the other night, why did you make an excuse and leave?' Gautier shrugged his shoulders, not wishing to give his reasons, and Sophia continued. 'You knew I was inviting you to stay the night, did you not?'

'I suspected so.'

'Were you shocked by my boldness? I cannot help it, Jean-Paul. Perhaps because I escaped from a country where women are little more than serfs, I believe that a woman should be free to show her feelings; just as free as a man.'

'You're right. I suppose I'm old-fashioned.'

'And this evening. Did you mind my telling the hotel proprietor that we wished to spend the night here?'

'I'm glad you did.'

She laughed as she leaned over to kiss him. 'Then if you're glad, for Heaven's sake show me you are!'

14

'Are you mad, Gautier?'

Although Courtrand's reaction the following morning when a pack of cards was laid on the table at their meeting was entirely predictable, Gautier still enjoyed it. In a way it was a small recompense for all the unmerited rebukes and reprimands he received. The other inspectors at the meeting were amused too. They were all older men and submissively obedient to the director-general out of concern for their pensions, but they admired Gautier's independence and occasional impertinences.

'The cards will help me to illustrate something which I have discovered about the affair of the Condemned Ones, Monsieur.'

Courtrand looked at him, suspicious of a hoax. 'And will they also tell us who is responsible for these murders?' he asked sarcastically.

'They may help us to identify the murderer.' Gautier spread the cards out on the table. 'It struck me that the choice of cards against each of the names on the list might have some mathematical significance, so I went to see Professor Racine.'

'Of the university?'

'Yes, Monsieur.'

'Did you know that he is married to a daughter of a former director-general of the Sûreté?'

'No, but he is a brilliant man.'

'That goes without saying.'

172

The fact that he was married to the daughter of a man as important as himself was, in Courtrand's eyes, a more convincing credential for Professor Racine than any university degree. He listened attentively as Gautier explained the properties of Pascal's triangle and then laid out the cards to demonstrate the trick Racine had shown him. Finally Gautier took out his copy of the list of Condemned Ones and made a pyramid of cards, showing how they fitted in with the order in which the people on the list were being attacked.

'A servant of Jacques Mounet named Desmarais has been missing for some days. If we assume that he has been murdered and that it happened before the Minister of Finance was stabbed, then the next victim would be represented by a five. That means either the deputy Claude Rozière or the Russian singer Ivan Grigov.'

'Then we must give them police protection immediately and for twenty-four hours a day.'

'I have already made arrangements which I hope will ensure their safety,' Gautier replied, and he told the meeting what he had done.

'And are they still both unharmed?'

'Grigov spent the whole of yesterday in his hotel and I have had no reports that anything happened there. I also telephoned the local police in the area where Rozière is staying and told them to keep an eye on him unobtrusively. If there had been any trouble they would have let me know.'

'In the circumstances what you did was not unreasonable,' Courtrand conceded grudgingly. 'But you should have kept me informed.'

'It was Saturday afternoon, Monsieur, and I thought you would be occupied with other matters.'

'I was, but I am never too busy to neglect my responsibilities.'

'Your theory of the mathematical pattern behind these attacks is plausible, Gautier,' one of the other inspectors said. 'It fits the facts. But how will it help us to identify the person who planned the whole affair?'

'It may not, immediately. But at least we know a little more about him. Whoever it is must have a knowledge of mathematics to be aware of Pascal's triangle. Most people would never have even heard of it.'

'Wait a minute,' Courtrand said, and then he turned to his secretary who was sitting beside him. 'Corbin, you have the dossier on this man Astrux. What does it say about his background?'

Corbin flicked through the dossier but Gautier sensed that he already knew the answer to his chief's question. 'Before turning to astrology, he studied mathematics. He has a university degree in the subject.'

'There you are!' Courtrand thumped the table. 'He has a knowledge of advanced mathematics and of playing cards.' He held up one of the playing cards as Galileo might have held up a sphere. 'I told you the scoundrel read my wife's future in cards.'

'In Gautier's report on the murder of the watchmaker Ribot,' one of the inspectors said, 'he mentions a book on astrology that was found in the dead man's apartment. Surely that is significant?'

'Book? What book?' Copies of the report Gautier had prepared had been circulated to all the inspectors but Courtrand had clearly not read his.

'It was a rare book dating back to the seventeenth century; a collector's book and not the kind one would have expected to find in Ribot's possession.'

'Then how do you suppose it came to be there?'

'It might have been given to him as payment for making that bomb. Less conspicuous than cash but an asset to be realised whenever it suited Ribot.'

'That proves it! Who except Astrux would have a book on astrology?'

'Any collector of rare books might.'

'Nonsense! We have our man.' Ignoring Gautier, Courtrand turned to one of the inspectors. 'Go immediately and arrest him. I will see that a *juge d'instruction* is ready to start interrogating him by the time you return.'

'We will need more evidence to get him into court.'

'And we shall get it, never fear. Once he realises how much we know, he may well confess. No, Gautier, we should have brought him in for questioning days ago, but you persuaded me not to against my better judgement.' Courtrand looked round the table. 'Are there any questions?'

'Yes, Monsieur. Why should Astrux want to kill all those people on the list?'

'His hatred of the president is well known and it was Judge Lacaze who conducted his trial for libel. You will have seen from Gautier's reports that Jacques Mounet wrote a defamatory article about him and he claims that Valanis stole a necklace from him. I have no doubt we will learn his motives for killing the others on the list in due course.' Courtrand sat back and looked at his inspectors complacently. 'Yes, Messieurs, I am confident that we will soon be able to wring a confession from this rogue.'

As he made his way back to his office, a sense of frustration filled Gautier. Before the morning was over Astrux would be brought before an examining magistrate and Gautier would be required to attend the examination. The process would be lengthy, continuing for days in all probability with Astrux confined in prison during the night. Gautier would be responsible for collecting him from prison every morning and returning him there in the evenings. Courtrand, meanwhile, confident that the case had been solved and the murders brought to an end, would withdraw police protection from Ivan Grigov and let Rozière know that it was safe for him to come back to Paris.

Intuition told Gautier that the murders would not necessarily end. It had yet to be proved that Astrux was responsible. If he were not, then whoever had planned the crimes would be free to continue his attacks. Eight people, more than half of those named in the infamous list, had now either been killed or attacked or had disappeared. Something must be done, and done quickly, to bring the affair to an end.

Back in his office Surat was waiting for him with news. The police had been trying to make an inventory of Ribot's property, listing what they had found both in his apartment and in his workshop to establish whether his murderer had stolen anything. The task had been made almost impossible, for Ribot, not surprisingly in view of his dubious activities and past associations, had not kept proper records or accounts and they had been forced to work on scraps of paper given as receipts for watches and clocks which he was repairing and anything else they could find.

'We had one stroke of luck,' Surat reported. 'A grocer from the *quartier*, as soon as he heard that Ribot was dead, came along to ask about his watch which he claimed he had left with Ribot. It was a fine gold timepiece his father had left him, and Ribot was to clean and regulate it.'

'And the watch is missing?'

'Yes. We could find no sign of it.'

'That could be useful. Ask the owner of the watch to give you as much information as he can about it – a full description, the name of the maker, any identifying marks.'

'There is another matter you should know about. The men who were sent to guard the singer Grigov in his hotel have been complaining.'

'About what?'

'His behaviour. They say he grew very truculent last night and insisted that he was going out. One of the policemen tried to follow him and says he went to rue de Richelieu. Apparently he was drunk.'

'Are you saying he went to a *maison closée*?' Gautier asked. Rue de Richelieu was known for its very high-class and luxurious brothels.

'The policeman believes so, but he lost him before he reached it. Anyway Grigov came back to the hotel two hours later. He appears to have come to no harm.'

'I will have to speak to him. Do you have anything else to report?' Gautier knew that Surat very often kept his most important piece of news to the last, not deliberately but because he did not appreciate its significance.

'There is one thing, but it does not seem to be connected with the affair of the Condemned Ones.'

'What is it?'

'There has been another murder in Pigalle. A woman this time, but she was killed in the same fashion as the two men who were knifed to death there – Ardot and Sandeau.'

The woman who had been murdered in Pigalle had been little more than a girl, seventeen at most and pretty but with the thin brittle body, pale complexion and flushed cheeks which suggested she was a consumptive. She had been a waitress at a large brasserie in Clichy, one of the Brasserie des Filles where the girls were more an attraction than the beer and available to those who were willing to pay the price. Her name, Gautier was told, was Jeanne Berton, but she had worked under the name of Yvette.

Yvette's body had been found in an alley, a dark slit between mean buildings in which the smell of stale urine was stronger than that of garbage, a slit almost as horrible as the knife wounds in her stomach. Her murderer had made a clumsy attempt to disembowel her, and Gautier, who had come to Pigalle readily, for it gave him a reason for escaping from the judicial examination of Astrux, was saddened and sickened by the sight of the young, mutilated body.

The reason why her death had not been reported earlier was that her killer had partly hidden the body behind some rubble and wood ripped out of one of the houses bordering the alley, where the floor of an upper room had collapsed only the previous week, killing two young children, and where builders had been working. As always a small group of people had gathered to stare at death, even though they were held back by a rope which the police had used to cordon off the place where the body had been found and it was hidden from their gaze by a sheet. Unusually for Pigalle there were people in the crowd who were prepared to help the police, and Gautier supposed it was because Yvette had been well liked and they were sickened by her death.

'When are you flics going to catch this monster?' a man at the front of the crowd shouted at Gautier belligerently.

'Not until we get a little help from you people.'

'What help can we give? Here in Pigalle we're only ordinary folk.'

'This is the third brutal killing in your *quartier*. There must be some among you who have information which would help us. You may have seen a man behaving suspiciously, heard a rumour in a café. The murderer must live somewhere, he may have a family, he must have acquaintances.'

'Someone did see him this time.'

'Who?'

'Old Bossu, the hunchback who sells shoelaces in the streets. He says he was almost knocked over by a man who came rushing out of here last night.'

'Where can I find him?'

'When he has money he drinks at the Café Soleil d'Or.'

The Soleil d'Or was the café which Suzanne and her lover Gaston had run while she was alive and to which Gautier had sent Surat a few days previously. This time he knew he could not avoid going there himself. He told the two policemen from the local commissariat, who had been at the scene of the murder when he arrived, to search the whole area thoroughly, particularly the building rubble, although he was not hopeful that they would find anything. Then, as the ambulance arrived to take Yvette's body to the mortuary, he left for the café.

Gaston's pleasure when he saw him arrive and the emotion in his handshake made Gautier ashamed that he could not find it in him to be friendly with the man.

'You've come on business, I suppose, Jean-Paul?'

'Yes,' Gautier replied, and saw Gaston's disappointment in his eyes.

'Well, you'll take a glass at least.'

Gaston poured two glasses of absinthe and Gautier could not refuse. He had never tried to acquire a taste for absinthe for he knew how much misery and degradation it had inflicted on the French people. One could buy a glass of the 'Green Fairy' as it was called for a sou, and it was the favourite drink of those who wished to deaden the squalor of their lives. Strangling a parrot was the popular expression for swallowing a glass of absinthe, and it had strangled the talents and destroyed the lives of many poets and artists.

'How is the boy?' Gautier asked Gaston. Suzanne had died giving birth to a baby son.

'Fine! My married sister in Créteil is looking after him, for the time being at least.'

'And the café? How is business?'

'Not bad at all. Some of those penniless artists from the Butte began to come down here. They would drink four or five bottles of wine and then say they could not pay for it. I had to put a stop to that.'

'I am here in connection with the death of that girl.' Gautier hoped that he had made enough polite enquiries to satisfy Gaston.

'Yvette? She lived not far from here with an Algerian. They came in sometimes.'

'People say that a hunchback claims to have seen the man who murdered her.'

'That must be Bossu. He's over there.' Gaston pointed towards the far corner of the café where a small hunch-backed man sat alone, lingering over what was left of a bottle of wine.

'Will he talk?'

'Perhaps, if I ask him to and if you buy him a glass. Come, I'll take you over to him.'

The hunchback looked up at them when they reached his table. He had small, malevolent but intelligent eyes and the fingers with which he was holding his glass were gnarled and twisted with rheumatism, more like twigs on a diseased branch of a tree.

'This is Inspecteur Gautier,' Gaston said, sitting down at the table and motioning Gautier to do the same.

'I don't talk to flics.'

'Don't you want to see the man who killed Yvette caught?'

Bossu thought about that for a moment. Then he said, 'I talk better when my throat isn't dry.'

Gaston had brought the absinthe bottle with them and he poured the hunchback a glass. He swallowed it in one gulp and held it out to be refilled. The liquid turned cloudy as he added water to the second glass.

'People say you saw the man who killed Yvette,' Gautier said to him.

'Saw him? He nearly knocked me over as he came running out of that alley. The swine! I lashed out at him with my stick but he was too fast for me.'

'Can you describe him?'

'It was dark and he was gone in a flash. I would have taken a longer look if I had known the swine had just slit that poor girl's stomach open. It was only today that I realised he must have been the one who did it.'

'Can't you tell me anything at all about him? Was he tall or short?'

'Tall. He was a big man.'

'Taller than me?' To the little hunchback all men would seem tall.

'No, shorter than you, but he was broad. And there was one thing I noticed. He was bald.'

'Are you certain?'

'Yes. He was completely bald. Even in the dark his bald skull gleamed, as smooth as an ostrich's egg.'

They talked for a little longer, but Gautier soon realised that there was nothing more that Bossu knew which would be helpful and that the man was merely dragging out the conversation so that his glass would keep being refilled. Leaving him, he and Gaston returned to the table where they had been sitting earlier, and as the absinthe was empty Gaston beckoned to the young woman who had been serving the other customers in the café to bring them another one. When she brought it, Gautier sensed from the way in which she looked at Gaston and the easy familiarity between them that the relationship was more than one of employer and waitress. Soon, if she had not done so already, she would be taking Suzanne's place in the rooms above the café where Gaston lived, and perhaps also as mother to Suzanne's child. The idea brought a sharp stab of resentment which he recognised as totally illogical.

'If Bossu is right, we should be able to find this character,' he told Gaston. 'There can't be so many completely bald men.'

'Agreed. I don't remember seeing one in my café.'

'It may take time though, especially if he comes from another *quartier*.'

Gautier had finished his second glass of absinthe and was about to leave, when one of the policemen whom he had left to search the alley where Yvette's body had been found came into the café. He was holding something in his hand which Gautier did not at first recognise.

'I found this among the bricks and rubble in the alley, Inspecteur,' the man said. 'It's a wig.'

181

The wig was obviously a cheap one, badly made and of poor quality, remarkable only for its colour. It was a strange colour for anyone to have chosen, a brassy yellow which would make the wearer far more conspicuous than even complete baldness. Gautier was reminded of the wigs he had seen worn by clowns in one of the many circuses in Paris.

On his way back to Sûreté headquarters, he began planning what he would do about this latest murder in Pigalle. In essence the operation would be the same as he had organised a few days earlier, with a team of police-men going out to make door-to-door enquiries, but this time they knew something about the man for whom they would be looking. The team would consist of fifteen men, if he could get them, and they would start in Pigalle and work outwards in a circle, visiting every café, bistro and cabaret. There were few Frenchmen who did not go into a café, and a very large proportion would go into one every working day, for a coffee and a marc on the way to work, for wine to drink with the lunch they took with them or for an aperitif and a chat with friends on the way home. Gautier was also debating with himself whether the policemen should not also call at shops selling food. He had the feeling that the murderer was probably a solitary, a man living on his own in a furnished room, and in that case he would buy food to cook for himself, possibly always at the same shop. Men allowed their lives to be dominated by habit to a much greater extent than women.

When he reached his office he sent for Surat and showed him the wig. 'Do you know any wigmakers?'

'No, but I can easily find one.'

'I want fifteen wigs like this one. They need not be identical in style but their colour should match as closely as possible. It will probably mean dyeing ordinary fair-haired wigs.'

'That should be simple enough.'

'And I want them ready by tomorrow morning. Pay whatever you have to.'

After Surat had left he began reluctantly to go through the pile of paper which had accumulated on his desk since he had left his office at mid-day. Mostly it consisted of reports written by the inspectors and policemen working on different aspects of the affair of the Condemned Ones. Many of the reports were outdated, already overtaken by events, for their copying and circulating was a slow, laborious process.

He found it difficult to concentrate, for Yvette's murder still nagged at him. As far as one could tell it was not connected in any way with the murders of the people on the list of Condemned Ones which had already been committed. The only name on the list which had still not been identified was Achard, and that was not Yvette's name. It was possible that she had been killed in error, mistaken for some woman named Achard, but that seemed unlikely. And yet there were similarities between her death and those of the two men killed in Pigalle, Ardot and Sandeau. The most plausible explanation was that her murder had been a deliberate copy of the other two, carried out by someone who had read the details of them in the newspapers. Crime had a curious imitative compulsion, and when there was a succession of identical murders it was not uncommon for some mentally unstable person, who might never previously have committed any crime, to attempt to imitate them. And yet that explanation seemed too facile to Gautier. He could not help feeling that he must have overlooked or misinterpreted some seemingly trivial fact which was essential to an understanding of the whole business of the Condemned Ones.

Meanwhile time was slipping away. As soon as police protection was withdrawn from Grigov and Rozière, the murderer's next target would be within his reach again and he would strike. He might not even wait for that. Even though Judge Lacaze had escaped injury from the bomb in his court and the Comte de Neuville's cook had survived the poison attempt, the murderer had continued with his attacks, as though a successful outcome in each of them was less important than executing them in their planned order. If that were the case he might by-pass Grigov or Rozière and aim for his next victim.

Pulling the pack of cards from his pocket, Gautier laid out the pyramid of fifteen which Professor Racine and he had constructed. Then he took away the bottom row of five cards and the row of four above it. He looked at the cards which were left.

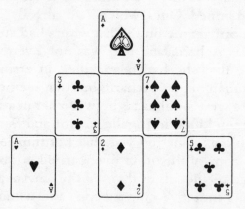

If his deduction was right, the next person to be attacked was the one represented by the ace of hearts on the left of the row of three cards, and that was Loubet, the President of the Republic. Alternatively, if he and Racine had placed the cards incorrectly, it could be that the ace of spades should be there and that Jacques Mounet was intended to be the next victim. A sudden thought alarmed him. If Courtrand was convinced that Astrux was responsible for the plot of the Condemned Ones, he might have told the President that his life was no longer in danger and the extra guards who had been put on duty, protecting Loubet day and night since his name appeared on the list, might have been withdrawn.

He hurried down to the director-general's office. Courtrand was not there for he had already left for the day to get ready for an important evening engagement. Most of his engagements were important enough for him to spend an hour having his beard trimmed and his moustaches curled. His secretary Corbin was, however, still at work in the tiny room next to Courtrand's office and he assured Gautier that no instructions had been given to abandon the special precautions that had been taken to protect the President. That would not be done until Astrux confessed or had been committed for trial.

When he returned to his office and began reading the pile of reports again, Gautier found a *petit bleu* among them that was addressed to him personally. It was from Michelle Le Tellier.

> The Duchesse de Chalon's masked ball is
> tonight and I shall expect you at eight-thirty.
> You should not need this reminder, but I know
> your attention is distracted by other things –
> and other women.

15

Before leaving the Sûreté, Gautier had been given a transcript of Astrux's interrogation that afternoon by the *juge d'instruction*, and while he was changing into evening clothes for the masked ball he stopped to read it for a second time. Astrux had performed badly, like a thoroughly frightened or a guilty man. The judge had concentrated his early questions on trying to make Astrux admit that he had paid Ribot to make both of the bombs that had exploded and that he was implicated in the murder of the watchmaker. As the examination continued the answers of the accused man had become confused and sometimes contradictory. First he had denied having even heard of the name of the book on astrology which had been found in Ribot's home. Later he admitted knowing of the book but denied having ever owned one. Finally he admitted having once owned a later edition of the book, but claimed that it had been either lost or stolen.

His replies to questions about his movements on the night of Ribot's murder had been even more damaging. At first he had said that he had dined with friends and returned home early, but he could not recall the names of the friends. Then he changed his story, saying he had dined alone, watched a performance of *Le Misanthrope* at the Comédie Française and then spent the night in a small hotel with a girl he had picked up in the gardens of the Palais Royal. He had not been able to give either the name or the location of the hotel.

Gautier did not believe that Astrux had been responsible for the murders. In his opinion the fortune-teller was not a man who would turn to violence. He made his living by his perceptiveness and with his tongue, calculating what people wished to hear about themselves and their future and then saying it plausibly and in phrases that suggested a supernatural revelation. If he were wronged or offended, he would wound with his tongue or his pen, not with a knife or a bomb. But he was caught now, trapped in the clumsy maw of the French judicial machine, which would not spew him out until he had given it a confession or irrefutable proof of his innocence.

Gautier was reassured to learn that the special precautions that had been taken to protect the President from attack had not been relaxed, but he did not overlook the possibility that the next intended victim might not be Loubet but Jacques Mounet. When he was leaving the Sûreté he had considered going to see Mounet, but had decided not to. From the outset Mounet had been clearly disturbed to know that his name was on the list of Condemned Ones and his nervousness had been turned into fear by what he thought had been an attempt to poison him and by the disappearance of Yussif. Mounet, Gautier was confident, would not expose himself unnecessarily to danger and needed no further warning.

As he continued dressing he found himself forgetting police business and thinking of the night he had spent with Princesse Sophia, and the memory brought a sharp, sensual excitement. They had made love as equals, neither dominating, neither submissive, each one demanding and giving in turn. He was not naïve enough to believe that what they had experienced was unique, but in his experience it was rare for two people to achieve such a complete fusion of pleasure and satisfaction in their first lovemaking.

When he was dressed he looked for his top hat and cane. The hat, he noticed, had not been ironed since the last time he had worn it, but he smoothed the nap with his sleeve and decided it would pass. There was an assortment of walking-sticks, umbrellas and canes in the umbrella stand, accumulated over the years. He was pulling out the black, silver-topped cane which he usually carried when he went out in evening clothes, when he saw another, similar in length and colour but larger in diameter and with a large silver knob. It was a swordstick which his father had owned and it stirred amused but affectionate memories. Supposing that a tax collector would not be a popular figure in a small, rural community, his father had bought the swordstick for self-protection and then never had occasion to carry, much less to use it. Gautier had never carried it either and as he picked it up he admired its workmanship. It looked like any other fashionable cane but, by sliding a small button below the knob, one could release the lock holding the two portions of the cane together. Then by pulling on the knob, which was in effect the handle of the sword, one could withdraw the blade that was sheathed in the length of cane below it. The blade, of Toledo steel, did not have a sharp edge but a thrust with its point would inflict a damaging wound.

On a sudden nostalgic impulse he decided he would take the swordstick that evening. As he set out walking towards rue de Grenelle, where he would be able to pick up a *fiacre*, he thought with wry amusement of what his father would say if he could see him. Although well satisfied with the life he had made for his family, his father had been ambitious for his only son, but he could never have imagined that one day Jean-Paul would be setting out in evening dress to attend the masked ball of the Duc and Duchesse de Chalon. Gautier was inclined to disbelieve it himself.

As he was walking along a narrow street, lit only by distantly spaced gas lamps, he heard a noise from in front of him which he did not at first recognise: louder and more irregular than footsteps, two thumps in quick succession,

188

followed by a pause. Then he saw the noise came from a man walking on crutches some distance ahead of him. The noise was the thump of the crutches on the cobbles of the street followed by the stamp of the one leg he was using. The other leg hung down limply, bent at the knee. He caught the man up and, as he passed him, formed the impression that he was coloured, although deliberately he did not look at him. Some poor devil wounded in North Africa, he thought.

He had walked on a few paces when he was suddenly alerted, sensing that something was wrong. Almost immediately he realised what it was. The thump of the crutches on the cobbles had stopped. He turned quickly and saw the man was moving up behind him, quickly and noiselessly, both crutches tucked under one arm. When he realised that Gautier had seen him he leapt forward, dropping the crutches, one arm raised. Gautier saw the knife gleaming in the light of a gas lamp and had time to raise his left arm, warding off the stab that was aimed at his chest.

He felt the blade plunge through his sleeve into his forearm and stepped backwards quickly before the man could attack again. In spite of the searing pain he was able with his left hand to slide the button below the knob of the swordstick and withdraw the blade, letting the bottom half of it drop to the ground.

The coloured man was standing with his back to the nearest street lamp and Gautier could not see his face. He seemed to hesitate momentarily, wondering perhaps what Gautier had done with his cane and not recognising a swordstick. Then he moved, poised for another thrust with his knife. Gautier lunged at him with the sword blade, aiming for the hand which held the knife. His aim was not perfect but it was effective and he felt the point of the blade make impact, piercing the flesh somewhere in the man's arm.

The man yelled with surprise as much as pain and leapt back. Then, when he saw the sword blade, he shouted an obscenity, turned and ran. Gautier listened as his footsteps echoed among the buildings on each side of the street.

When the maid who opened the door of Michelle Le Tellier's apartment saw Gautier, she screamed. The sleeve of his coat was slashed, blood had poured down over his wrist and hand, and in his other hand he was carrying his hat and cane, with two crutches tucked under his arm. As he stepped into the apartment, a drop of blood fell on the polished wooden floor, and when the maid saw it she screamed once more.

Michelle looked out round the door to her bedroom and Gautier saw she was not fully dressed. 'Mother of God! What's the matter?' she called out to the maid, and then she saw Gautier. 'Jean-Paul! Is this some joke?'

'I wish it were. A man attacked me with a knife on my way here.'

At first she did not believe him. Then, suddenly remembering that she was not fully dressed, she went back into her bedroom and came back wearing a *peignoir*. Gautier had taken off his coat and when she saw his tattered, bloodstained shirt-sleeve, she gasped.

'It isn't as bad as it looks,' he told her. 'I had to tear a strip from my shirt to bandage my arm.'

'I'll send for a doctor.'

'That won't be necessary. The bleeding has almost stopped.'

'But the wound must be stitched.'

'It can wait till tomorrow; or at least until later tonight.'

'You cannot possibly go to the ball like that!' Michelle had forgotten about the Duchesse de Chalon's ball, and now, as she remembered, he saw dismay in her eyes.

'I can and I will. Is one of your maids a good sempstress?'

'My cook is – exceptionally good.'

'Then ask her to stitch up the gash in the sleeve of my coat.' Gautier handed the coat to the maid. 'The blood will have to be sponged off.'

'There is blood on your trousers as well.'

'I shall take them off presently and they can be sponged and pressed as well. The only problem is the shirt. Where will I be able to buy one at this time of night?'

'Heaven knows,' Michelle replied, and then she hesitated before adding, 'Most of my husband's clothes are still in the wardrobe of his dressing room. There will be evening shirts among them and he was about your size. Would you object to wearing one?'

'Of course not.'

Gautier knew that Michelle probably expected that he would object to wearing her former husband's clothes; she might believe that he should mind, but he had never felt any jealousy for her husband or for the life they had shared. Retrospective jealousy had always struck him as a singularly futile emotion. He had never even met Le Tellier.

Between them, and with the help of the maid and the cook, they managed to give his appearance at least a veneer of respectability. The sleeve of his coat had only been slit by the knife and the cook's stitching was scarcely visible, while after the maid had ironed them his evening trousers looked smarter than they had before.

'You're not intending to take those crutches with you, are you? It would be the first time I danced with a man on crutches, although some of the men I know might dance better on crutches,' Michelle said gaily. Now that she was assured that they would be going to the ball, she was in a good humour.

'No. I shall leave them here if I may and have them collected tomorrow.'

'We should have got a pirate's mask for you, one with a bloodthirsty expression and a patch over one eye.'

191

Michelle had bought masks for both of them to wear to the ball. Gautier had supposed that they would be simple masks, covering the eyes and no more, like the mask that a harlequin traditionally wore, but the Duchesse de Chalon had told her guests that she was expecting more. Their masks should really conceal their faces and at the same time be amusing, a substitute for fancy dress, for dressing up in elaborate, comic outfits was tiresome and inelegant. So Michelle had bought Gautier a mask of a Chinaman with long drooping moustaches, while her own was one of a cat's face with a grin and whiskers.

As they were being driven to the ball in her coach, holding the masks in their laps, she suddenly said, 'Admiral Pottier will be there tonight?'

'Will he?'

'Yes, and you should be prepared in case he is rude to you. Poor Theo! He's not very good at disguising his feelings.'

'What would he be feeling?'

'Jealousy, I suppose.'

'Why on earth should he be jealous?'

'He has been very attentive to me lately.' Michelle looked away as she replied, coyly, as though to hide a blush. In the darkness, Gautier could not make out whether she was blushing.

'So it's your turn now?'

'I don't know what you mean, but it doesn't sound very gallant.'

'The admiral has a reputation as an incurable phi-landerer.'

'Perhaps he was, but those days may be over.'

The remark sounded as though it were meant to be enigmatic, but Gautier could think of only one plausible explanation for it and for why Michelle had raised the subject of Admiral Pottier at all. He said nothing, for to ask her whether the explanation was the right one would have been both blunt and presumptuous.

'Theo was with me last night,' Michelle continued, and then, as though to answer his unspoken question, she added, 'but what he really wants is to marry again. It is ridiculous for a man of his age to be running around after women. Poor Theo! Do you know that after his wife died he moved out of their lovely house in Faubourg St-Germain and allowed his married daughter to live there? Now he lives alone in a wretched little *garçonière* just behind Quai d'Orsay. He's very lonely, of course.'

'And will you marry him?' There seemed to be no way of avoiding the direct question.

'Why not? Being a widow on your own is very difficult in society. And Theo comes of a good family. He is still a person of importance in France.'

They rode on in silence for a time, with Michelle thinking perhaps of how she would be able to persuade Pottier to relinquish the pleasures of his second bachelorhood. Gautier, for his part, was thinking of the change he had observed in Michelle. While she had been in mourning for her husband and they had dined together clandestinely at her home, he had been impressed by her conversation, her culture and her knowledge. She had opened windows for him on to music and literature, poetry and the theatre. Now she seemed interested only in the preoccupations of society life. He recalled the eagerness with which she had absorbed the gossip of Madame Mauberge's salon, the petty spite of her remarks about Princesse Sophia. She reminded him of a person returning from a religious retreat during which her attention has been concentrated on spiritual matters, who, as soon as she re-enters the everyday world, is carried away by its trivial pleasures.

And recognising the change in her, he also noticed that he felt neither disappointment nor regret. That could mean only that his affection for her had been no more than superficial, and he found himself wondering, as he often had before, whether he had the capacity to form a deep and lasting relationship with any woman.

'I knew you would understand, Jean-Paul,' Michelle said, laying a hand on his arm and squeezing it. 'You're so sympathetic.'

'That is always the talent of the man who finishes second,' Gautier replied. It was the remark he would be expected to make, and as he made it he wondered where the border between courtesy and hypocrisy lay.

'Are you certain you feel up to going to the ball tonight?'

Gautier's arm was still throbbing painfully, the sleeves of the shirt he was wearing were absurdly short and the collar too tight, but he was prepared to endure a little discomfort, not because he would enjoy the ball but because the timing of the attack on him by the man with the crutches convinced him that the evening would have an important part to play in the plan of what he no longer thought of as the affair of the Condemned Ones but as Murder by Numbers.

16

The Duc and Duchesse de Chalon lived in a large house which had been built for them in Boulevard de Courcelles, when they were married fifteen years previously. The architect had been determined to outshine the other splendid homes that had been built for wealthy bourgeois families in the last two decades of the nineteenth century, and everyone agreed that he had succeeded. A wit had observed that the house was grand enough to become a museum when no one could afford the expense of maintaining it, and he was probably right.

The duchess had a surprise for her guests at the ball that evening. A Brazilian who had brought an immense dowry to her marriage with the elderly, fragile duke, she was fond of surprises and, because she spent her money extravagantly and well, her surprises were as popular as she was. On this occasion her surprise was to give her ball as its theme *A Thousand and One Nights*, a choice inspired by the recent publication of a French translation of the Arabian tales.

She and the decorator she had engaged to help her had been carried away by their enthusiasm and their imagination. A canopy of blue silk, decorated with crescent moons and silver stars, had been suspended beneath the ceiling of the ballroom, so that one had the feeling of being in a vast tent erected in the desert, an impression which was reinforced by the lengths of brightly coloured silk hanging from the walls. In other rooms, divans and ottomans were piled high with cushions, crossed scimitars had been fixed to the walls and the vases filled with peacocks' feathers.

Even the servants had been attired to match the décor. The maids who admitted guests to the house and took the gentlemen's hats and the ladies' stoles wore what the duchess believed was worn by concubines in a harem, and had their faces concealed behind yashmaks. As a final fantasy a band of muscular waiters had been engaged to masquerade as eunuchs, waiting on the guests stripped to the waist, their skins stained brown with walnut juice, their heads shaved, wearing huge earrings, baggy trousers and gold sandals. The orchestra also wore Arabian dress but fortunately were not required to play music from the Levant.

The guests were received by the duke and duchess in the library, where they were asked to put on their masks and to keep them on until midnight when, at a stroke of a gong, all masks should be removed. The purpose of the masks was to add mystery and gaiety to the ball, with men inviting ladies anonymously to dance, much guessing of identities and risqué flirtations. Only the duke and duchess would not wear one.

As he looked around the ballroom, Gautier decided that the guests had shown a good deal less imagination than their hostess in choosing their masks. He saw a dozen or more Chinamen, several Satans with horns and pointed beard, three or four circus clowns and at least two *polichinelles* from the *guignol* puppet theatre. Among the ladies there were a score of Japanese geisha girls, numerous Red Indian squaws, fairy-tale princesses with red cheeks and flaxen plaits and masks of kittens, fawns and mice.

Michelle and Gautier had been in the ballroom for only a few moments when a tall man, who Gautier guessed must be Admiral Pottier, came up and asked Michelle to dance. The admiral was wearing a mask which was meant to represent Neptune, the god of the sea, with flowing locks among which small fish were entwined. It was obvious that Michelle must have told Pottier beforehand what mask she would be wearing, and probably what dress she would choose to put on, for he came up to her directly and without hesitation.

Gautier was not sorry to be left on his own, for he needed time to think. Instinct told him there would be drama at the ball that evening. A masked ball provided an almost perfect opportunity for a murder or an assassination. Once he had identified his victim, the murderer, disguised by his mask and by the anonymity of evening clothes, could fire his revolver or use his knife and disappear into the crowd of guests without being recognised. The murder could be done in seconds, and if he was to prevent it Gautier must do something more than stand and watch and wait for it. The first thing to do was to discover whether any likely victims were at the ball that night.

Leaving the ballroom, he made his way to the library. The duke and duchess were still there, receiving the last of their guests as they straggled in. Waiting for an opportune moment, Gautier approached the duchess, taking his mask off briefly to show who he was.

'Madame, would you mind telling me if Monsieur Jacques Mounet is among your guests here this evening?'

The duchess looked concerned. 'Oh dear! Is that an official question, Monsieur Gautier, or a social one?'

'Which would be more agreeable to you, Madame?'

'You reply to a question with a question.' The duchess rolled her eyes in mock despair. 'Then it must obviously be an official question. Does it mean that we should expect trouble?'

'Not if I can prevent it.'

'It is so reassuring to have you here, Monsieur Gautier, so very reassuring. Yes, Jacques Mounet is here tonight. He is quite unpredictable, that one! Wherever he goes, dinner parties, soirées, weddings, even funerals, he insists on dressing up in those ridiculous Byzantine robes. But tonight, when everyone else is disguised, he comes in conventional evening dress.'

'Could it be that he wants us to recognise him?'

'If that remark means that you are about to ask me what kind of mask he is wearing, don't! I forbid it!'

'I would never knowingly ask you anything which might embarrass you, Madame,' Gautier said, although that was exactly the question he had intended to ask the duchess.

She may have regretted her strictness, for as Gautier was leaving the library she called out to him, 'If it is of any interest to you, Monsieur Gautier, Jacques Mounet has brought his cousin Pierre with him tonight.'

Back in the ballroom Gautier reflected that knowing Mounet was among the guests did not solve the problem facing him. One must assume that the murderer's next victim might be any of four people: Grigov or Rozière or, if the murderer had decided to bypass them, President Loubet or Jacques Mounet. Since the only one of those four present at the ball was Mounet, Gautier would have to concentrate on giving him what protection he could, but that was possible only if he could identify him. Having reached this conclusion, he still had the uneasy feeling that his deductions might be wrong. Once more he found himself wondering whether there might be something he had overlooked, some fact which, if seen in its proper context, would put an entirely different complexion on the Murders by Numbers.

Presently Michelle and Pottier returned to join him, and almost immediately Michelle was asked to dance by another man whom Gautier did not recognise but who was wearing a Chinaman's mask not unlike his own. Pottier stared at the man belligerently and then, when they were alone, directed his hostility towards Gautier.

'I get the impression, Gautier, that you have been plaguing Madame Le Tellier with your attentions.'

'Madame Le Tellier and I have been friends for some time,' Gautier replied, 'and she has never complained that I pester her.'

'Well, this friendship must come to an end, do you hear?'

'Surely that is for the lady to decide.'

'As I have told you before, a word from me could wreck your career, Gautier.'

'Threats, Admiral? I thought you preferred violence to threats.'

'What are you talking about?'

'I recall our conversation when you wanted to have Paul Valanis assaulted.'

'Valanis?' The admiral seemed disconcerted. 'I never mentioned his name.'

'It isn't important.' Gautier was finding the conversation tedious. 'Anyway, you need not concern yourself with me as a rival. Madame Le Tellier has made it plain to me that she prefers your attentions to any I might pay her.'

'Really? She said that?' Pottier asked. Then he added haughtily, 'I should think so too.'

As he watched him walking away, Gautier decided that his original assessment of Pottier's character had not been proved wrong. The man was arrogant, headstrong and vain, but those were faults not uncommon among Frenchmen of Pottier's background and upbringing. They need not have been a handicap were it not for the fact that he was stupid as well.

He was looking around the room, trying to guess which of the many men there might be Jacques Mounet, searching for someone of the right height and build, when one of the waiters approached him, offering a tray laden with glasses of champagne. As he took a glass he noticed the man smile.

'You don't recognise me, Inspecteur.'

'Should I?'

'It's Duclos. I've worked for you more than once.'

Gautier realised then that he was a policeman from the Sûreté, a likeable young man, efficient and with a good sense of humour. 'My apologies. Your disguise is too good.'

'It certainly is! When I came out of the bedroom with this stuff on and in these clothes, my wife screamed that an Arab had broken into the house.'

'What are you doing here?'

'The duke asked for two policemen to be here tonight and suggested that they should come disguised as waiters. He was afraid there might be trouble.'

Gautier was not surprised by what he heard. In his time he had been sent more than once to big social functions to watch out for thieves or pickpockets. 'What kind of trouble?'

'Two kinds. A man who had not been invited threatened to come anyway. The duke was afraid he would make a scene.'

'Do you know his name?'

'I don't remember it, but they say he's an astrologer and a magician.'

Had he been asked, Gautier could have told the duke that Astrux would not be visiting him that evening, for he was in prison.

'And what was the other trouble they are expecting?'

'There was an anonymous message to say that a bomb had been planted in the house.'

Duclos told Gautier that he and his colleague from the Sûreté had searched the house thoroughly and found no bomb, nor had anyone so far tried to force their way uninvited into the ball. Gautier asked him no more questions but let him leave to circulate among the guests with his tray of champagne. If the man was to continue passing himself off as a waiter, he should not be seen talking for too long to a police inspector.

Gautier also began to mingle with the guests, looking for Jacques Mounet. As Mounet had been so alarmed to hear that his life was threatened and by what he imagined had been an attempt to poison him, it seemed surprising

200

that he should have exposed himself to danger by coming to the masked ball, but he had at least been prudent enough to come wearing evening dress rather than his Turkish robes. The author was a small man, not more than one metre seventy at the very most, and that would help, enabling Gautier to eliminate a very large proportion of the men in the ballroom. He tried to guess what kind of mask Mounet would be wearing; something distinctive in all probability, for the man was vain enough to wish for his to be different from the masks that other men would be wearing: not the mask of a Chinaman or of a circus clown. Admiral Pottier, another vain man, had chosen a mask of Neptune, the god of the oceans, believing no doubt that it symbolized his preeminence as a sailor. If Mounet gave in to his amour propre he would make a similar choice, the mask of a lion perhaps, for he was one of the literary lions of the day. But Gautier could see no lions.

Then, as he was walking along the fringe of the ballroom, he saw, dancing with a woman wearing the mask of a geisha girl, a short man wearing one of the sphinx. He felt a sudden excitement. The sphinx, surely, would appeal to Mounet for its connotations of omniscience, inscrutability and aloofness, and even more for its associations with life in the Middle East which Mounet so much admired. He would have liked to get close enough to the man to overhear his conversation and see whether he recognised the voice as that of Mounet, but he could only have done that by dancing and he could see no women standing nearby whom he might ask to partner him.

So he waited until the dance was over and then tried to follow the sphinx as he left the floor with his partner, hoping he could move closer to them. Luck was against him, for when the music stopped the sphinx was at the far end of the ballroom. As quickly as he could he worked his way through the crowd of dancers coming off the floor, but by the time he reached the end of the room the sphinx was nowhere to be seen. Leaving the ballroom, he went through the main drawing room, the smaller sitting room of the duchess and the other anterooms, in all of which guests were standing or sitting, talking and drinking champagne. Facing Gautier on all sides were batteries of masks: comic, sad, gruesome or just commonplace, but no sphinx.

The dining room of the house was imposing, large enough to seat at least thirty and with glass doors opening on to a long conservatory filled with ferns, shrubs, orange trees in tubs and palms, some of them reaching to the glass roof. Gautier went in, thinking that other guests might be there, enjoying a few minutes of privacy among the plants. At first he saw no one, but he heard voices coming from beyond a batch of palms. The woman's voice he recognised at once as that of Princesse Sophia; the man's voice also had a slight foreign accent, but it took him some moments to realise that it was Paul Valanis speaking.

He kept on walking, for instinct, trained by many years of police duty, told him that if his footsteps were suddenly to stop Valanis and the princess would become aware of his presence. He had the feeling too that he should not deliberately eavesdrop on their conversation, but could not avoid hearing a fragment of it.

'Are you suggesting that I should become a party to this plot?' he heard Princesse Sophia say.

'Why not? You are the ideal person,' Valanis replied.

'I'm sorry. I could never agree to do what you ask.'

'If you did, a large sum of money would be donated towards the expenses of the opera company they say you plan to bring to Paris next year.'

'That's bribery!' Sophia said indignantly.

By this time Gautier had moved away and he heard no more of what they were saying. He was curious to know what kind of proposition Valanis had been making to Sophia, and equally curious to know whether they had met in the conservatory by arrangement; if not, he wondered how Valanis would have recognised her. Passing through the dining room he found a place in the room beyond from where he could see both pairs of glass doors leading to the conservatory. He waited there, and presently both Sophia and Valanis came out separately, using different doors.

Sophia was wearing a yellow dress, trimmed at the sleeves and neck with pale blue and with its full skirt gathered up to one side with a large blue bow. Instead of a mask she had put on a yashmak of blue silk, just as effective as a disguise and far more elegant. Gautier knew at once that he would have recognised her in spite of the yashmak, and as he looked at her he felt a resurgence of the excitement she had aroused in him the previous night. Their awakening that morning and the return to Paris from Asnières had been practical, not sentimental. They had driven to the city in a *fiacre* and Sophia had laughed when Gautier had suggested that they should travel separately so that she would not be compromised.

'What an old-fashioned creature you are!' she had teased him. 'I appreciate your concern for my reputation, but really I don't mind who knows that we slept together last night.'

Now Gautier watched her as she went through the dining room and then followed her as she made her way to the ballroom. When she reached it she stood looking around her as though uncertain whether she should join one of the groups of people who were standing at the edge of the room. As he approached her she looked round and immediately held out her hand to be kissed.

'Jean-Paul! I was wondering where you were.'

'How did you recognise me?'

'I am not sure. Perhaps you send out vibrations, these waves through the atmosphere which Signor Marconi talks about.'

'You look as though you had lost someone,' Gautier observed.

'In a way I have. My escort this evening has vanished.'

'He must be mad if he leaves you on your own.'

As he made the remark, Gautier remembered that the friend who was supposed to be dining with the princess after the races at Longchamp had also failed to appear. He found it surprising that such a beautiful woman should be so neglected by her male partners.

'And you? What are you doing here on your own?' Sophia asked.

'The lady I was escorting has been swept away by a handsome sailor.'

'So we have been thrown together once more. Do you think it is the hand of fate?'

'Who knows? We will have to ask the Great Astrux.'

'Why, is he here tonight?'

'Sadly for him no. He is in the St-Lazare prison.'

'My God! Why?'

'He is being interrogated in connection with the bomb that exploded on the houseboat of Paul Valanis.'

The name of Valanis was clearly one which the princess had no wish to hear. She had expressive eyes which responded readily and engagingly to her moods, to amusement, pleasure, eagerness. Now for an instant they glinted with irritation, and Gautier thought she was about to tell him of her argument with Valanis in the conservatory. If she had intended to, she thought better of it.

'I have the suspicion, Jean-Paul,' she said, 'that you did not come to the ball for amusement. You have the air of a man with a problem on his mind and that, I suppose, means a criminal problem.'

'I may be worrying without cause, but if there is any possibility of a crime I like to prevent it.'

'What kind of crime are you thinking of?'

As she was speaking, Gautier noticed that the man in the sphinx's mask had returned to the ballroom and was standing in a group of people not far from them. As he studied the man he became convinced that it was Jacques Mounet, so instead of answering Sophia's question, he said, 'Evidently you have a talent for guessing the identity of masked men. Do you think the man with the mask of a sphinx there is Jacques Mounet?'

She looked in the direction to which he had pointed. 'What reason have you for thinking that he is?'

'No reason really. It is no more than a guess.'

'How badly do you need to know?'

'If it is Mounet I may be able to save his life.'

Sophia looked around her until she saw one of the eunuch-waiters who were serving the champagne. She went up to the man, they exchanged a few words and he handed her his tray on which there were still several tall, fluted glasses of the sparkling wine. Gautier found himself wondering, for no reason at all, whether the *marque* of champagne they were drinking was Edward VII's favourite.

Taking the tray, Sophia began walking round the room offering it to the guests, exactly as the waiters were doing. Gautier realised that she intended to offer a glass to the sphinx so that if he spoke she would be able to tell from his voice whether it was Mounet. He admired her astuteness. As he waited he glanced round the room. There were several waiters at work serving the guests, but he could not see Duclos. One of the men, he noticed, was dressed differently from the rest, wearing in addition to the baggy pantaloons a short tunic open down the front like a bolero, but with sleeves. He supposed that the man must be some kind of head waiter or supervisor, for he did not seem to be working himself but simply watching to see that all was well. Did they have a chief eunuch in a harem? he wondered.

When Sophia reached the sphinx, she held the tray out to him and to the people with him. Gautier saw the sphinx hesitate, as though he were uncertain whether she was in

205

fact a waitress or a guest playing a joke. He took a glass, but did not appear to speak to her. Then, to Gautier's surprise, she did not return to him, but continued on her way round the room. Then he understood the reason for her prolonging the masquerade. At the far end of the room there was another man wearing an identical sphinx mask. When she reached the man, Sophia offered him her tray and he took a glass of champagne, saying something to her as he did so. Sophia did not stay to talk to him but came back to Gautier, making a detour to return the tray to the waiter from whom she had taken it.

When she reached Gautier she said, 'You did not tell me there were two men here disguised as the sphinx.'

'I did not know there were.'

'The first one certainly was not Jacques Mounet.'

'How could you tell?'

'By his smell, or rather the lack of smell.'

'What do you mean?'

'Have you not noticed how the smell of tobacco or hashish or whatever else it is that Jacques Mounet smokes in his hookah lingers on him? In his hair and on his clothes? It's unmistakable.'

'Then what about the second sphinx?'

'Oh yes, he's Jacques Mounet. Apart from the smell, he spoke a few words to me and I'm certain I recognised his voice.'

Gautier looked at the two sphinxes. The men were similar in build, both short and well-developed and with hair of the same colour. 'If the sphinx at the far end of the room is Jacques Mounet,' he told Sophia, 'then the other one must be his cousin Pierre. As long as they wear those masks it will be impossible to tell them apart, not from a distance anyway.'

'There is one way of distinguishing between them. Pierre Mounet is wearing a white carnation in his button-hole.'

'I wonder why,' Gautier said, thinking aloud.

Sophia shrugged. 'Perhaps so that he will not be mistaken for Jacques.'

'Holy Father!'

Gautier gasped. Sophia's casual remark exploded like a starting pistol, releasing his mind to race away, the barriers which had held it back suddenly no longer barriers but signposts, and as he raced he saw at the end of the course truth, simple and, for Gautier, beautiful as the solution to any baffling puzzle always was. He knew, though, that he did not have the time to stand back and admire it.

'Shall we move closer to Pierre Mounet?' he suggested to Sophia.

'Why? Do you wish to speak to him?'

'No, to hear him speak. I have to be sure that it is him behind that mask.'

They moved towards the nearer of the two sphinxes, sauntering casually and as though deep in conversation, although Gautier was scarcely aware of the platitudes they were exchanging. As far as he could tell, neither the sphinx nor anyone else was taking any interest in them. When they were only a few paces away they stopped, and Gautier could hear the voice of the sphinx. He knew then that it was Pierre Mounet. Mounet was with a couple whom Gautier did not recognise and he was telling them about his invitation from King Edward VII. The visit to Cowes was going to be the high point of the man's life and he could not be blamed for telling people about it.

Gautier was trying to decide whether they should join Mounet and his companions and what he should say to him if they did, when Sophia remarked, 'I believe your other sphinx is coming to ask me for a dance.'

'Why do you think that?'

'When I offered him champagne he paid me an extravagant compliment. He seemed to be quite taken with me.'

'Who would not be? But if he does ask for a dance, please put him off.'

'Yes, my lord. A well-trained concubine always obeys her master.'

When the second sphinx reached them he bowed and asked Sophia if she would give him the pleasure of a dance. She replied that the next dance was already promised and then, studying her programme, offered to put him down for the fourth dance from then. Her reply seemed to satisfy the sphinx, who bowed again and left them. As they were talking, Gautier had sniffed surreptitiously but could not detect the odour which Sophia had described. All he could smell was her perfume. He knew from the man's voice, though, that it was Jacques Mounet.

'He kept glancing in my direction,' he told Sophia. 'I wonder if he recognised me.'

'Would it matter if he did?'

'I'm not sure.'

Tension was mounting inside him. He sensed that the drama he had been expecting at the ball was imminent and that it would be a drama of violence. He had no means of knowing when and with what weapon the author of the drama would translate his carefully contrived plan into reality. The orchestra began to play once more, a Viennese waltz this time, and he saw that Pierre Mounet had asked the woman next to him to dance.

'Shall we dance?' he asked Sophia.

They joined the other dancers and as they waltzed Gautier followed Pierre Mounet and his partner, trying to keep as close as he could to them. It was not easy, for Mounet was an energetic dancer, moving swiftly and sweeping past other couples as he swung his partner round. Gautier was certain that danger was imminent. Now was the perfect moment for a murderer to strike, with the sound of music to drown a pistol shot and the rapid movements of so many couples to cause confusion. He

had the feeling that he was living a nightmare, surrounded by leering, masked figures in a macabre dance
of death.

He needed help. As they danced he looked around the
ballroom, hoping to see the man from the Sûreté, Duclos,
but the only other eunuch he could see was the one in the
tunic, the head waiter as he had thought. Once more the
man was not doing any waiting, but stood at the front edge
of the guests who were standing round the room, only a
couple of metres from where Pierre Mounet had stood
talking before he started to dance.

This time the truth stunned him. The waltz was ending,
the music rising in a crescendo in the final bars. Quickly
he spun Sophia round in three extra steps which took
them beyond Pierre Mounet and his partner. The music
stopped, and as they started to leave the dance floor they
were on Mounet's left.

'Say something to the sphinx on your right,' he whispered urgently to Sophia. 'Anything.'

She did as he asked, making a remark which he could
not hear. Mounet stopped for an instant to listen to what
she was saying and to reply. Gautier was watching the head
eunuch and he noticed the man reaching into the pocket
of his pantaloons. When Mounet stopped, he hesitated, but
only for a brief moment, and then he began to withdraw
his hand from his pocket.

Leaping forward, Gautier grabbed the man, encircling
his body with a hug so that he could not move his arms.
The man shouted with pain and, staggering back, fell to
the floor, taking Gautier with him. Struggling violently,
he managed to free one arm and pulled his hand out of
his pocket with the revolver he had been holding. At once
Gautier grabbed his wrist with both hands. For several
seconds they wrestled, the muzzle of the revolver swinging
from side to side. If the trigger had been squeezed almost
anyone near them might have been shot. Then, as Gautier

twisted his arm, the man screamed with pain and let the revolver fall.

'Somebody help me!' Gautier shouted.

No one moved. The people nearby had backed away and were staring at the two of them with horrified fascination as they wrestled. A woman screamed. Then another eunuch forced his way through the crowd and Gautier saw that it was Duclos. A few seconds later the second policeman from the Sûreté arrived, and between the three of them they held the man captive, still struggling and shouting obscenities.

'Take him into another room and keep him there,' Gautier told the two policemen.

His mask had slipped down on to his neck, and as he pulled it off the Duchesse de Chalon came hurrying up, looking shocked and anxious and followed by her husband. 'Tell the orchestra to start playing again, Madame,' Gautier told her.

'What's happening?'

'Let your guests think it was just a drunken brawl.'

When he recognised Gautier, Pierre Mounet took off his own mask. 'Inspecteur Gautier! What was that man intending to do?'

'He came here to shoot you, Monsieur.'

'But why? Who is he?'

'When the colour has been wiped from his face, I think we shall find he is a Breton sailor named Lucien Desmarais.'

17

The two men from the Sûreté had taken Desmarais to the duke's study, which was some distance from the ballroom, and where they would not be disturbed by inquisitive guests. The duke and duchess accompanied Gautier there, together with Pierre Mounet and Princesse Sophia. On his way to the study, Gautier sent one of the waiters to Admiral Pottier, asking him to join them. There was a telephone in the study and he used it to call Sûreté headquarters, asking for a police waggon and more men to be sent to the duke's home.

The scene in the study, which had also been decorated in the same style as the other rooms in the house, might have been one from an oriental fantasy, with two coloured eunuchs holding a third prisoner. Desmarais had given up struggling and stood sullen and defiant between the two policemen. The left sleeve of his golden tunic was stained with blood. When Gautier went and pulled the sleeve up, he saw a bandage had been bound around the wound which he had made in the man's arm with his swordstick and which had started to bleed again.

'Who is this man?' the Duchesse de Chalon asked.

'The personal servant of Jacques Mounet,' Gautier replied.

'Should Jacques not be here?' Pierre Mounet asked.

'I should be surprised if he did not arrive at any moment.'

Gautier was right. Before he had time to say anything to Desmarais, Mounet came hurrying into the study. He had taken off his mask and in conventional evening dress was no more than an ordinary man, small and in no way worthy of notice. Gautier wondered whether this was the reason he masqueraded in oriental clothes so often, to hide his insignificance.

'Yussif, is it really you?' Mounet stared at Desmarais in disbelief.

'Don't pretend that you did not know it was your servant, Monsieur.'

'What has he done? Why is he being held prisoner?'

'He has murdered one man and had he not been prevented he would have killed another tonight.'

'Who?'

'Your cousin.'

'I cannot believe that. Why on earth should Yussif wish to kill Pierre?'

'Because you asked him to.'

Gautier's accusation, loud and unequivocal, caused a sensation, as he had expected it would. Everyone in the room stared at Jacques Mounet, waiting for his response. Before he could make one there was a diversion as Admiral Pottier came into the study accompanied by Michelle Le Tellier. His manner was one of belligerent anger.

'I have come here against my better judgement, Gautier,' he said loudly. 'How dare you send me orders?'

His blustering was ignored, for everyone's attention was taken by Jacques Mounet. Pierre Mounet said to Gautier, 'There must have been some mistake, Inspecteur. It is inconceivable that Jacques should have wished to have me shot.'

'One can understand your disbelief, Monsieur, but it's true. Your cousin devised a most elaborate plot, warning the police anonymously that several people were to be assassinated. And he put his own name on the list, so that when you were shot we would assume you had been mistaken for him.'

'I still cannot believe it.'

'Tell me, was it his idea that you two came to the ball tonight wearing identical masks? Masks which he had specially made, no doubt, so that no one here would be wearing a similar one?'

'Yes, but—'

'Only Desmarais here would know which of you was which. He knew you would be wearing a white carnation.'

Pierre Mounet looked at his cousin in surprise. 'Jacques! Where is your buttonhole?'

'I see,' Gautier commented. 'He provided carnations for both of you and then, some time after you arrived here, got rid of his. Neat!'

The self-assurance which Jacques Mounet had displayed when he came into the study was ebbing away, and one could see an uneasiness in his eyes. He had come to defend his servant if he could and was disconcerted not only to find himself suddenly accused, but also by the confidence with which Gautier confronted him.

'This is ridiculous!' he protested. 'You told me the other day that several people on the list you received were already dead. Are you accusing me of having them killed as well?'

'No. Your list of Condemned Ones was drawn up after four of the people on it had been killed, two by some madman in Pigalle and two by the bomb which exploded on the houseboat in the Seine.'

'In that case, whom am I accused of having murdered?'

'A watchmaker named Ribot who made a bomb for you and took it to the Palais de Justice, and a footman in the service of the Comte de Neuville. You and Desmarais will also be accused of the attack on the Minister of Finance at Longchamp races and of attempting to murder me.'

Everyone in the room was silent. Their initial surprise had been overtaken by a more complex emotion, and they were watching Mounet without pity, curious to see whether he could struggle free of the net which had been thrown over him.

213

Only Pierre Mounet was still incredulous and confused. 'Why should Jacques wish to harm me? He has no reason for hating me.'

'No?' Jacques Mounet's question was a whiplash, vindictive and stinging. He could not restrain the pent-up bitterness of thirty years and more. 'Your father stole my father's share of their business, leaving us destitute, leaving my father to kill himself and my mother to live in poverty for the rest of her life. And you say I have no reason for hating you!'

'It isn't true!' Pierre Mounet was shocked by the viciousness of his cousin's words.

'I have no doubt it isn't,' Gautier said. 'But he believed it was true and that was motive enough.'

'And as soon as my mother dies,' Jacques Mounet said, trembling with anger, 'worn out by drudgery and privation, you get your reward, the final accolade, an invitation to go yachting with the King of England.'

While he was talking two uniformed policemen came quietly into the study. They were from the Sûreté and Gautier knew this meant that the waggon for which he had sent must have arrived. He nodded to the men and they crossed the room and stood one on each side of Jacques Mounet. When they went to hold him, he shook himself free angrily. He was ready to accept arrest but was determined to leave with dignity. The two policemen led him out of the room and Desmarais followed with the two eunuchs.

'Jacques must have hated me all these years,' Pierre Mounet said after they had left. He still appeared bewildered.

'Yes, and when his mother died grief turned his hatred into venom. He was waiting to revenge himself on you and when he learnt you were coming to Paris to supervise the repairs to the houseboat, he worked out a very ingenious plan to kill you.'

'Then it was not he who put the bomb on the houseboat of Paul Valanis?' the Duchesse de Chalon asked.

'No.'

'Who did?'

'Admiral Pottier.'

The second sensation which Gautier created that night was even more devastating than the first. Pottier was a member of the *gratin* by right, born into society, while Jacques Mounet was a member, some might think an interloper, admitted only on the doubtful passport of literary talent. One of the women in the room gave a short, hysterical laugh. Pottier was unprepared, thinking himself safe perhaps when he saw Mounet arrested.

'Is this a joke?' he demanded.

'You stole a rowing boat from a boatyard on the Seine not far from where you live,' Gautier continued, 'and used it to take your home-made bomb to the houseboat.'

'This man has got to be stopped.' Pottier turned to the other people in the room. 'Is he allowed to accuse everybody?'

'I was crossing Pont Neuf on my way home after a night on duty. I saw you rowing away from the houseboat, a minute or so before the bomb exploded. You crossed the river and carried on towards Notre Dame. If you had looked round you would have seen me,' Gautier said, and then he added, 'You were wearing a brown suit and a brown derby hat.'

Panic overwhelmed Pottier. Like a bird trapped in a room his mind darted from one point to another, searching for an escape, but speed of thought was not one of his gifts.

'Theo, how could you? Two sailors were killed by that bomb.'

Michelle Le Tellier's reproach destroyed Pottier. His face, his whole personality, seemed to crumble with despair. 'I did not know there was anyone on board,' he said.

215

'Michelle, I would never kill innocent sailors. I was one myself. You know that.'

Justifying himself to Michelle, excusing his actions to her, was more important to him than denying his guilt. Gautier realised that the man must be genuinely fond of her.

'Why did Jacques Mounet work out such an elaborate plan to murder his cousin?' Sophia asked Gautier.

'He had to make us believe that when Pierre was murdered he had been mistaken for himself.'

'Could he not simply have sent himself an anonymous letter threatening his life?'

'If he had, we would have given him police protection which would have made it that much more difficult for Desmarais to kill Pierre. As it was, we thought the President was to be the next victim and so of course our attention was concentrated on him.'

The night was warm enough for Sophia and Gautier to walk by the river at Asnières. They had dined at the Hôtel de Paris and had decided to take a stroll before going to their room. For the previous few days they had seen little of each other, with Gautier immersed in the seemingly endless formalities needed to prepare the cases against three men who would be tried for murder.

The evidence to support the charges against the three had been painstakingly assembled. In the small hotel in which Lucien Desmarais had been staying after he had left Jacques Mounet's apartment, the gold watch missing from Ribot's workshop had been found hidden on top of a wardrobe. The book on astrology found in the watchmaker's apartment had been traced to a dealer in rare books, who was ready to testify that he had sold it to Mounet. Admiral Pottier had been careless enough to leave part of the equipment he had used to make his bomb in his *garçonnière*.

There was other evidence, some of it circumstantial, which would be used in court. A nurse in a small hospital run by a religious order had dressed the wound in Desmarais's arm which Gautier had made with his sword-stick. He told the nurse that he had been dressing for a fancy-dress ball and had accidentally stabbed himself with a pair of scissors. The Duchesse de Chalon had told the police that it was Mounet who had persuaded her to organise her masked ball on the theme of *A Thousand and One Nights* and who had put her in touch with the caterers who had supplied the waiters. A coachman of a *fiacre* had identified Pottier as the man he had picked up near Notre Dame and driven to Quai d'Orsay early in the morning on the day when the bomb had exploded on Valanis's houseboat.

'Why did he make such a long list of names?' Sophia asked. 'And why the bizarre idea of the playing cards?'

'He wanted us to think that the assassinations were the work of a group of people, anarchists perhaps. I am not sure of the reason for the cards. He may have thought that playing cards would point our suspicions towards Astrux. There were people on the list, remember, whom Astrux hated: the President, Mounet and Judge Lacaze.'

'And Paul Valanis.'

'Valanis was a piece of luck, a bonus if you like. Mounet would not have known that Valanis had taken Antoinette's necklace back from Astrux by force.'

At first Gautier had been inclined to dismiss Mounet's use of playing cards and a pyramid of numbers based on Pascal's triangle as mere bravura, typical of the man. Mounet's arrogance would demand a complex, unusual plot. On reflection, he realised that its purpose had been more subtle. By mystifying the police it would distract attention from Mounet's real objective, and if eventually they guessed the significance of the pyramid of cards they would still not be certain who the next victim was intended to be because of the duplication of numbers.

'I should have realised much sooner what the murderer had in mind,' he told Sophia. 'Mounet's plan was not original. Others in the past have arranged a succession of apparently motiveless murders just to conceal the identity of the one person they really wished to kill.'

'How could anybody be so callous?'

'Mounet was not callous enough. He did not have the stomach for undiscriminating violence and wished to avoid killing anyone if he could, apart from his cousin. The first four men on his list were murdered by somebody else. They were already dead when he made the list.'

'How did you know that?'

Gautier explained that Villon, one of the sailors killed on the houseboat, should not have been sleeping on board that night and only took the place of his friend at the last minute. Mounet must have taken his name and the names of the men killed in Pigalle from reports in the newspapers.

'And the bomb in the law courts was timed to explode when Judge Lacaze would not be there, the poison Mounet put in the Comte de Neuville's cognac was not enough to kill any healthy servant who might drink it and when Lucien stabbed Risson-Vernet he meant to wound not to kill him.'

'But they killed the watchmaker.'

'That was only after the plan began to go wrong. Ribot was recognised in the law courts. It was sheer bad luck, a chance in a thousand. Lucien killed him because they were afraid he would give them away when he was being questioned, and he tried to make it appear as though Astrux had done it.'

And the gold watch in Ribot's workshop had been another piece of ill luck, as Gautier knew. Desmarais had not been able to resist taking it, and when confronted with the fact that it had been found in his hotel room he had

218

confessed to murdering Ribot. He had taken the watch, he said, because he had always wanted one. Gautier could not help wondering why Mounet had never given him one and what the outcome would have been if he had. As it was, one could see quite clearly what would happen. Desmarais had not yet confessed to attacking Risson-Vernet, but eventually he would. He would try to shield Mounet but would fail. Mounet would be too proud to let his servant go to the guillotine for him.

'Do you think they intended to kill you?' Sophia asked.

'I don't think so; just to wound me so that I would not be at the masked ball. Mounet must have discovered that I was to be among the guests.'

They stopped walking and stood looking across the river. A mist hung over the water, not dense enough to snuff out the lights on the far side but reducing them to a pale, ghostly glimmer. Gautier was reminded of the times when, as a boy in the country, he had seen the moon break out from behind drifting clouds surrounded by a kind of halo, a sure sign that there were storms at sea that night, he had been told. His arm was around Sophia's waist, her arms round his, and when he kissed her once more her lips were open, her response eager. He felt desire stirring and with unspoken consent they turned and began walking back towards the hotel.

They passed a houseboat tied up by the bank of the river, an old hulk, but still in use, for they could see a light shining inside it, the home perhaps of river folk or a bargee. A very different boat from the luxurious *Antoinette*, it must still have reminded Sophia of Valanis.

'Paul Valanis invited me to go on a cruise he plans to make in his boat.'

'Does that mean he is tired of Admiral Pottier's granddaughter Antoinette?'

'Not at all. He is not interested in me. His idea was that I should chaperone Antoinette. He seemed to believe that her parents would not refuse to let her join the cruise if she was to be chaperoned by a princess and that Pottier would not dare to interfere. I think he guessed that it was Pottier who had bombed his boat.'

Gautier was pleased that she told him what Valanis had proposed to her in the conservatory during the masked ball. He had been curious to know, but had he asked her he would have shown that he had been listening to their conversation.

'Did you really see Theo in a rowing boat on the Seine that morning?' Sophia asked.

'I know now it was the admiral. At the time I did not recognise him.'

'You said he was wearing a brown suit and brown derby hat?'

'That's right.'

She stopped walking and faced him. 'I was wearing a man's brown suit and hat when we met in Astrux's consulting rooms. God in Heaven! You suspected me of putting the bomb on the houseboat!'

'It was a possibility I had to explore. And you had reason for hating three men whose names were on the list of Condemned Ones: Mounet and Grigov and Fleury.'

'I have never been suspected of murder before.' She laughed, took his arm and began walking again.

Gautier wondered whether he ever really had suspected her. Since its dramatic dénouement at the Duchesse de Neuville's ball, he had thought critically more than once of his handling of the case. When he first went to see Jacques Mounet and told him that his name was on the list of Condemned Ones, Mounet had lied. He had pretended that he did not know his cousin was in Paris, but by then he had already sent Pierre a note offering to help him enjoy his stay. People lied for all sorts of reasons, very often trivial reasons: vanity, pride, to avoid embarrassment. The great majority of lies were innocent enough, and because

Mounet's name was among those whose lives were being threatened, Gautier had thought no more of it. He should not have been so naïve.

When they were in their room at the hotel and began to take off their clothes, he forgot about Mounet. For most women undressing was a slow and tedious process, with many layers to be removed, skirts, underskirts, corsets, much unbuttoning and untying, but Sophia accomplished it effortlessly and quickly. But just before she was naked, she suddenly stopped.

'When did you decide that I was not involved in your murders?' she asked.

'When I watched you trying to row.'

She stared at him, her face a ring in which surprise wrestled with indignation and indignation with disbelief. 'So that was why you brought me to the *guinguette* last Sunday! It was just a plan to test my innocence!'

Gautier hoped that his smile was not as shamefaced as he felt. 'That was not the only reason,' he began.

He need not have worried about explaining his motives. Sophia's anger, if she had felt any, evaporated at once, and she began to laugh. She laughed loudly and without restraint, her hands on her hips, her head thrown back. When at last she was able to stop, she put her arms around his neck.

'Now I understand why you would not sleep with me that night at my home,' she said. 'You were too honest. I love you for that, Jean-Paul.'

After they had made love, and as the sharp ecstasy subsided, Gautier felt a twinge of regret. Their journey from Paris to the hotel where they had first made love, the dinner, the walk by the Seine, the return to the same room which they had shared before, seemed to make the occasion no more than an adventure, sentimental and banal. He had slept with other women, had his share of casual affairs and now the memory of them devalued a night which, for her sake as well as his, he had wanted to be much more.

'Michelle Le Tellier will come back to you now,' Sophia said. 'Will she not?'

'No, she never would.'

Sophia's remark showed that, in spite of her cosmopolitan and sophisticated life, she still saw emotional situations in simplistic terms, loving and hating, conquest and surrender, jealousy and indifference. In Gautier's experience life was seldom as clear-cut as that. Michelle Le Tellier was a proud woman. Gautier had shown no anger or resentment when she told him she intended to marry Admiral Pottier, and now that Pottier had been disgraced she would never forgive him for that.

'Would you not like to marry again?' Sophia asked.

'I have never given the idea much thought.'

'You could marry me.'

Gautier stared at her in astonishment. Now it was his turn to laugh. He laughed so loudly and for so long that the guests in the next room of the hotel to theirs rapped on the wall in reproach.

'Why do you laugh?'

'Can you hear them announcing us as we arrive at a soirée? "Inspecteur Gautier and the Princesse Sophia"? What a sensation that would create!'

'I would drop my title, of course. Take that away and what have you got? A children's nurse.'

She began trying to convince him that there would be nothing outrageous in their marrying. Her second husband, whom she had met at a health spa, might just as easily have been a businessman as a prince. She and Gautier were of the same bourgeois stock. That was one reason why they understood each other, why they had found an immediate rapport.

When she saw that her arguments were making no impact, she said, 'In a few days I am leaving for St Petersburg, but I will be back next year. I am going to make Paris my

222

home. While I am away will you think about what I have suggested? Promise me you will.'

Gautier knew that he would have to discipline himself not to think about marrying her. Fantasies were only a substitute for reality, and they were dangerous, for they could become addictive. Next morning he must start work again, going up to Pigalle, where there were three murders as yet unsolved. The net was closing around the bald-headed man now and there were reports that he and his yellow wig had been seen. Even so, he would think of Sophia.

He could give no promise, make no commitment, but he wanted at least to tell her that he would think of her, often. But when he looked at her he saw that her eyes were closed and could tell from the change in the pattern of her breathing that she was asleep.